MOD

Michèle Nayman was born in London but grew up in Johannesburg and Melbourne. She has worked as a journalist and marketing executive in Australia, South-east Asia and Europe. She now lives in London. *Somewhere Else*, a collection of short stories, was published by Heinemann Australia. *Jetlag* is her first novel.

Other 90s titles

jetlag

a novel

michèle nayman

This volume was published with assistance from the
Ralph Lewis Award at the University of Sussex

Library of Congress Catalog Card Number: 93–87447

A CIP record for this book is obtainable from the
British Library on request

First published in 1994 by
Serpent's Tail, 4 Blackstock Mews, London N4; and
401 West Broadway #1, New York, NY 100012

Set in 10½/14 pt Goudy by Intype, London
Printed in Great Britain by Cox & Wyman Ltd, Reading, Berkshire

part one: asia

chapter one

Some memories are so vivid you can spend years scanning them, as if searching for clues.

The fog had started to lift. I leaned over the wall of the rooftop garden in Jardine's Lookout and watched the towering apartment blocks of the Peak come into view through the mist. It was like watching a photograph develop. There it was: Victoria Harbour at dusk. And there I was, October 1982, a new beginning.

"Who do you think you are – Ruby Tuesday?" Olivia Bates had asked me at a press conference to mark the opening of yet another new hotel in Tsim Sha Tsui East the day before.

She would never say where she came from. Ruby Tuesday, the Rolling Stones song of the Sixties, had been my secret anthem, but I'd never said this to anyone, not even to Susan Roth, the friend who'd introduced me to the song in Melbourne. I'd certainly never mentioned it to Olivia.

"I've told you where I'm from," I said.

"That's not what I mean," Olivia replied.

Yesterday don't matter if it's gone.

Olivia smiled, but a little too late.

She was smiling now as she joined me to look at the view. "I'd introduce you to Steven," she said, "but he doesn't appear to have come back from the wine shop. I'll see if he's downstairs."

She made her way through a wrought-iron gate. I turned

around and watched as three tall, fair-skinned men tinkered with a gleaming new barbecue. One of them leaned awkwardly to peer underneath.

"Those three never were much good with hardware," said a man of my own age wearing a white windcheater, ORION emblazoned in silver letters.

"The problem is they haven't got a manual," someone else offered.

"Maybe they forgot to put the software in," said the first man. "Hey," he yelled across the garden, "any of you Scots thought to use a light?"

One of the Scots grimaced and held up a box of matches. Everyone on the roof laughed.

Olivia re-emerged through the gate, followed by a ginger-haired man with ginger eyebrows and a ginger moustache. He was wearing a T-shirt and shorts, yet he walked with a bow-legged formality that gave the odd impression he was wearing a suit.

"Steven Reid, meet Laurie Michaels," Olivia said.

I held out my hand. Steven seemed surprised, but his hand-shake was strong. He smiled, bobbed his head up and down several times, and made a sweeping gesture with his arm. "This may look like just another flat to you," he said, "but it's the first real place I've had in two years. I've been living at The Excelsior since August. Before that, it was hotels in the Middle East. Anyway, welcome. I'm glad Olivia invited you."

I reached into my shoulder bag and held out the gift-wrapped package I'd bought at Daimaru. "For your new home," I said.

Steven unravelled the ribbon, tore at the paper, opened the box, and held the small white teapot in freckled hands. He smiled again, hazel-amber eyes beneath drooping eyelids.

With those eyelids and that ginger hair, he looked for all the world like an earnest, eager spaniel.

"You mean you and Olivia are competitors?"

"Sure," I said. "What's strange about that?"

Steven scratched the back of his head. "I'll never understand journalists. I assumed you were colleagues."

"In a way we are," I said.

"But you work for *Asian Business Today* and she works for *Business Weekly*."

"We write about the same things – airlines, hotels, the tourism business in general."

"But why has she introduced you to her contacts, if you're competitors? I'd be out of a job if I did that. Adam would think I'd lost my mind. It doesn't make sense."

"You don't have to worry about Olivia," I said. "She has given me just enough to start finding my way and to become an amusing adversary. The only person you impress with a scoop is your opposite number at a rival publication. You think anyone else notices? In any case, her magazine is based here. Mine is published out of Singapore."

"Still doesn't make sense."

I laughed and glanced around The Excelsior's coffeeshop. "Neither does inviting me for a meal in a hotel you were so keen to leave."

"I got used to this place," he said. "I sort of miss it."

The meal arrived and we discussed other things. But, when the waiter cleared the main course away, Steven said: "What we talked about earlier confirmed what I've always suspected about journalists."

"What's that?"

"That their agenda is different from what they say it is. My policy – professionally speaking – has been to steer clear of journalists."

The hazel-amber eyes had become wary.

"My policy," I said, "professionally speaking, has been to steer clear of computer salesmen."

"Orion Constellation is not a computer as such," he said. "It's a computer system. For project management. You probably don't know what that is."

"As it happens," I said, "I do. Construction schedules. Job cards. Just-in-time inventories for materials."

"How do you know that?"

"I studied town planning at university."

"Really?"

"Really."

Steven lowered his eyes in embarrassment hastily concealed. When he lifted them again, the spaniel look had returned and he grinned. "How about an ice-cream, then?" he asked, his Geordie accent becoming more pronounced. "There's chocolate – not as good as at The Regent, but not bad; there's caramel, which is the best in Causeway Bay; but what I recommend most – you should try it, truly, is . . ."

"You can't stop selling, can you!"

"I'm proud of what I do," he said.

"So am I."

We stared at each other. To defuse the hostility, I ordered the ice-cream he had recommended – cappuccino and rum – and, to be fair, it wasn't bad at all.

Hotel coffeeshops: I grew to like them as much as Steven did. I had breakfasts in them – sumptuous affairs of fruit, yoghurt and pancakes at The Regent with contacts on expense accounts; more modest coffee and croissants at The Furama or The Hilton with newly acquired friends. I often had lunch in them, and dinner too, although having the hotel industry as part of my beat ensured a reliable stream of invitations to press conferences and briefings inevitably accompanied by banquets or cocktails. Business was done in Hong Kong over food.

And what food! Chefs from all over China competed with Australian, Swiss and French chefs in the top restaurants. On their days or nights off, they would eat at the hotels or restaurants of their competitors. They would pronounce judgement, perhaps learn something, bitch about kitchen hierarchies, and gossip about chefs whose soufflés or love-lives had fallen flat.

I loved the constant social buzz and the late nights at the office, filing stories to the news desk in Singapore. I loved the burr and blur of neon signs that left smudges in winter fog as taxi drivers sped manically past in the unspoken race that Hong Kong was – everyone rushing to the next customer, the next deal, however humble or unlikely to eventuate. Each day held great possibilities, even if only a chance to win at mah-jongg.

In 1997, only fifteen years away, Hong Kong was to revert to China after ninety-nine years of British rule. The brain-drain and the outflow of capital had begun, of course, but there was still huge money to be made, and businesspeople who had moved to the United States, Canada, or Australia to qualify for passports or permanent residency returned to Hong Kong as soon as they had completed the minimum requirement of stay. They talked of the boredom of exile and of the abominable food. They had transferred their personal assets and the registrations of their companies to places with more secure futures, but they weren't going to leave their beloved Hong Kong until they absolutely had to. When it came to business, pace and style, the rest of the world was light-years behind.

This was the image of Hong Kong that was fed to the world by people like Olivia and me. Other aspects of Hong Kong went largely unreported. "To you, second sister," Bindy Chung, the bookkeeper at the magazine, said to me one day after lunch, "1997 is the name of a nightclub and an interesting time. In 1997, you and the other Westerners, you and the rich Chinese, will all be gone. The rest of us – the small potatoes – will still be here. We'll be part of China and we'll have to take what comes our way."

Stung by shame, I'd been unable to reply. When I repeated Bindy's comments to Jerry Sokolov, vice-president, Asian operations, for International Travel Services Inc., he looked at me quizzically and puffed on his cigar. "This may sound unkind," he said, "and I don't mean it to be, but you have to choose between being a social worker or being someone who knows how to cut the end off a cigar. I shouldn't have to be telling you that – in Hong Kong, of all places. That's what Hong Kong was founded on. That's what Hong Kong has always been about."

I didn't know how to reply to Jerry, either. "I don't smoke cigars," I said, belonging neither to Bindy's world nor to Jerry's. I belonged somewhere in between, or perhaps nowhere at all. Everything moved so quickly in Hong Kong. It was difficult not to get a sense of falling behind. And so rushing about became my style, too, although it became clear quite quickly that moving at double speed didn't result in twice as much getting done. "It's the illusion of movement," I said to Olivia, who pointed out with her Cornish pragmatism that the phrase wasn't accurate. "The movement is real," she said. "What you mean is that getting things done is illusory."

We had been standing at the circular bar of the Foreign

Correspondents Club in Ice House Street listening to the usual contingent of Old Asia Hands talk of Saigon, Phnom Penh and Vientiane. Little had happened in the world in general and journalism in particular since the Vietnam War, if you were to believe the men – and they were all men – who told stories to one another and stared into their glasses of whisky or beer. When Saigon had fallen in 1975, most of the correspondents had gone home or to bureau postings elsewhere. The men who were standing around the FCC bar now, however, had stayed in Asia. These were Westerners for whom being a foreigner meant being at home, and often the other way round. Many of them had married Vietnamese, Cambodian or Laotian women and, despite the loneliness that cross-cultural marriages so often seemed to engender, they no longer found Western women – "round-eyes" – attractive. We were too large, too brash, too demanding, they said. I had noticed this attitude in expatriate businessmen I'd interviewed for *ABT*. I'd also seen the despair in the eyes of their wives.

Olivia and I were disturbed by the fear we saw behind that despair – the fear those women had of losing their men and the world to which those men gave them access. Olivia and I judged our lives and our worth in terms of our work, not through association with a man. We were journalists, our yearning for adventure urgent and fresh.

But, at the FCC, Olivia always got slightly depressed. "That war talk – " she said once, putting down a glass of Scotch so emphatically that it spilled. "The implication is that we're just playing at journalism, that the exciting times have been and gone."

"Their whole generation feels like that," I said, thinking of Susan, my friend and colleague at *The Age* in Melbourne.

Susan was eleven years older than Olivia and I were, and

seemed to be in permanent mourning for the Sixties. Susan had marched against Australia's involvement in the Vietnam War; had had dozens of lovers ("freedom begins with the body"); and had believed that conscience and the sheer strength of individual will would abolish social injustice. When the wide-ranging visions of the Sixties gave way to the Me Decade of the Seventies, Susan had turned inward, like everyone else, and had taken up Transcendental Meditation. She disliked the Eighties. They lacked the excitement of the Sixties, she said. This was where our age difference showed. The Eighties seemed exciting to me.

"Excitement is like luck," I said to Olivia. "We have to make our own."

"Oh Laurie," she laughed, "you sound like Steven Reid."

"What do you think of the Sixties?" I asked Steven.

"They're gone," he said.

"But what do you think of them?"

"Is it necessary to think of them? I have trouble remembering what happened last week. There's too much going on *now*. But, if you really want to know what I think, the Sixties were self-indulgent and shallow."

"But do you sometimes wonder," I persisted, "if a certain sense of excitement has been lost?"

"Excitement is what you make of things yourself."

I smiled. "Olivia was right."

Steven's face went blank while he weighed up whether or not I had insulted him.

"What I meant – what Olivia meant – was that you take a positive view of everything," I said.

"Why is that bad?"

"Did I say it was bad?"

"Look," said Steven, pushing a plate of mussels away, at our table in the corner of the Sheraton coffeeshop, "I grew up in a very different environment from Olivia and you. In my part of Newcastle, it was the factory or the mines. My father was in the factory all his life. Still is. My mother stayed at home, like all the other mothers. Still does. I wanted to be a professional soccer player. Football was the passport out.

"But we can't all be Kevin Keegan. So I did well at school instead, and was accepted at university. Only one other person in the class got a place – my best friend, as a matter of fact. We did electrical engineering. We couldn't think of what else to do. It never occurred to us that we could become doctors or lawyers. The home, the factory, the soccer field – that was the world."

"I grew up thinking the university was the world," I said. "I thought everyone's parents worked in the history department. I assumed I would, too."

Steven sat quietly but alert.

"I don't talk about this much," I said.

"I know. Olivia calls you Ruby Tuesday."

I smiled. "I imagine you don't much care for that song. There's nothing more Sixties than Ruby Tuesday."

"The history department," he said.

"I use that technique when interviewing, too," I said. Steven waited, unperturbed.

"You must be effective at what you do," I said. I looked at him, looking at me, but did not feel uneasy. There was a straightforwardness about Steven that put everyone he met at ease. He was not a handsome man – the impression of a spaniel had grown stronger each time I'd seen him – but his seriousness and interest in what was going on around him made him attractive, alive.

"I did start out in history, as it happens," I said. "But

I wanted something you could touch. I transferred to the architecture faculty and ended up in town planning. When I graduated, though, I went back to my old dream of being a journalist. Journalism, for me, was a licence to ask. *The Age* took me on as a graduate cadet. At first, I specialised in urban affairs, then state politics. Here, I've turned myself into a business reporter. I wouldn't mind a coffee."

Steven got the waiter's attention, and ordered for both of us. I would have been better off without another cup of coffee – I'd had too many cups during the day and would have difficulty sleeping, again – but Steven was relaxed, and I wanted to hear more about who he was. "That brings you pretty much up to date with me," I said. "Over to you."

"I don't talk much about this, either," he said.

"Ginger Wednesday, then?"

He shook his head and grinned, the skin around his eyes gathering into extravagant etchings. I had a sudden urge to kiss him.

"I hated electrical engineering," he said. "Wires, currents, fiddly bits. Drove me mad. I finished the course only because I couldn't bear to admit I'd made a mistake."

The coffee came, and some chocolate mints.

"I stumbled into an MBA course," Steven said, dipping a mint into his coffee. "You don't mind if I do this, do you?"

"Get away – I'm an Australian."

"Too bloody right, mate," he said, and grinned.

"You mimic my accent too bloody well," I said. "Get on with the story."

He leaned forward. "I love pushy women."

"Steven!"

He leaned back again. "Most of my classmates became stockbrokers and management consultants. I enrolled in a PhD with one of the lecturers we'd had, an old leftie, passionate about types of social and economic control. My topic was the sociological effects of new technology."

Steven put down his cup. "The South of England was prospering, and the North – my half – was going down the tubes. The old industries weren't benefiting from new technology in the way that newer industries were in the South. I had some crazy scheme of explaining the social effects of all this."

He went silent.

"Social effects."

"Ah yes," he smiled, "the prompt."

"I'd like you to continue."

"I couldn't get it together," he sighed. "I spent nine months on it – the most miserable time of my life. The topic was unmanageable – for me, anyway. I realised, too, that I don't have a footnote mind. And then, suddenly, I saw what I wanted to do."

"What?"

He looked directly at me. "Make money."

"Oh," I said, unable to hide my disappointment.

"That probably sounds crass to you. Where I grew up, it wouldn't sound crass at all – merely impossible. The Sixties were never-never time. All those affluent kids – all those affluent *American* kids, shoving mom and pop aside for a while and dropping out – were people who knew they could find a slot again anytime they chose. In Newcastle, the problem was always how to drop *in*, any way at all.

"As for your Sixties nostalgia buffs – Olivia has told me about your FCC crowd – who think that nothing has happened since 1975, you should tell them to open their eyes. I've been in Saudi Arabia the past two years. Whole *cities* are going up there. When I arrived, there were no telephones. You had to get into your car and drive to who you wanted to see and hope he'd be there. If you wanted to fly somewhere, you had to drive to the airport and stand in a queue. If there were too many people ahead of you, you had to come back the next day.

"That was 1980. Then, almost overnight, Saudi got telephones, and the airline offices got computer booking facilities. One day there was nothing at all, the next day there was state-of-the-art technology in *everything*. It's the most amazing place I've ever been.

"Vietnam? Helicopters. Self-importance. And you wonder why I've so little time for journalists." He jabbed his finger in the air. "What's so great about war? What's so great about destruction? Orion Constellation systems are helping build oil rigs for the North Sea. They're helping build oil refineries and gas liquefaction plants throughout South-east Asia. They're being used on maintenance for aircraft, and on the NASA space shuttle. Why aren't those journalists writing about all that? The Vietnam War finished seven years ago."

"The ramifications have only just begun," I said lamely.

"Then why aren't those heroes of Olivia and yours out there reporting them? What do they think they're achieving by hanging around the FCC with their bullshit reminiscences of the Vietnam War?"

I didn't know what to say.

Before I'd come to Hong Kong, it had been rare for me not to know what to say. My life had been orderly and safe. My parents made their living from putting the past in order and passing it on. My sister was about to qualify as a doctor; my brother was studying agricultural science. Both of them had high ideals. My estranged husband was an architect who, like most architects trained in the Sixties, had been strongly influenced by Le Corbusier's philosophy of buildings as machines for living in. I was a journalist who believed in the usefulness of information and the public's right to know. I'd been happy in my marriage and in my profession of being licensed to ask. But an inexplicable restlessness had taken hold, and I'd left everything to come to Hong Kong. The only person who had seemed to know why was Susan Roth, who understood everyone except herself.

Susan had organised what were probably the world's last feminist consciousness-raising groups. She still meditated and did yoga. When friends came to her for advice – which they did, often – she listened, then gave them chicken soup, hash cookies, and sensible suggestions. Susan the pragmatic Jewish earth mother was also a talented journalist who spoke for the powerless – prisoners, mothers on benefits, the mentally ill.

I missed her. I wanted to ask her: How do you reply to Bindy Chung? How do you reply to Jerry Sokolov? How do you reply to Steven Reid?

I rang Susan several times the following few days. She wasn't at home. She wasn't at *The Age*. Someone there said something vague about Susan having taken time off. Perhaps she was avoiding me. She'd been unusually quiet when I'd told her I was going to work as a business reporter in Hong Kong. I'd taken her silence as approval. Perhaps I'd been wrong.

I went home to my small dilapidated flat in Mid-Levels, on the first floor of a building earmarked for demolition. I sat on the floor and stared at the lightbulb. It was time to buy lightshades and chairs.

At dinner in Repulse Bay not long afterwards, in a restaurant that isn't there any more, I looked out of the window at a grey sea and felt cold. I hadn't expected Hong Kong to be so cold. Steven also was looking at the sea, and a silence had settled between us which made me wonder if we'd reached the end of the things we had to say to each other.

Steven had been in Seoul for three days, talking to prospective customers. I'd spent those evenings at the FCC listening to more tales of Saigon, but with disillusioned ears. I still hadn't bought anything for the flat. I was camping in my own home. It didn't feel like my home – that was the problem. Steven, on the other hand, had furnished his flat in less than two weeks. The curtains matched the couch. There were stereo speakers in the lounge and the bedroom. There was a cupboard full of climbing boots. His salary was a lot higher than mine, I told myself, but that was just an excuse.

So here we were, a woman of twenty-six and a man just turned thirty, eating minced pigeon with lettuce leaves on a Saturday night in a large restaurant filled with smartly dressed Chinese families, the children immaculately well-behaved.

There were six English and Scottish boys of about sixteen or seventeen sitting at a table in the corner, making an elaborate show of being bored. But their knees and wrists were rigid; they appeared to be waiting.

The front door of the restaurant flung open, and in walked nine large Chinese youths dressed as American cowboys. They swaggered over to the British boys' table. One of the cowboys said something in Cantonese, and the largest of the British boys, a Scot, held up his hand in a gesture of warning. The Chinese boy repeated what he'd said, and the Scot swung his fist into the side of the boy's head, causing the Chinese boy to stagger, but only momentarily. The Chinese boy pulled out a flick knife. The Scottish boy did the same, and they faced each other, electric with adrenalin, uncertain what to do next.

Members of each gang spat insults at one another in Cantonese while the leaders maintained their positions with the knives. The Chinese families busied themselves with chopsticks. Waiters became statues.

Steven pushed back his chair and stood up. He walked across the room to the boys with the knives and stood between them. He was shorter than each of them but he held himself erect, his legs apart and his shoulders loose. He said something no one else in the restaurant could hear. The boys continued to watch each other. Steven stood there silently, his arms by his sides.

After five minutes, perhaps even longer, the leaders put their knives away, and the Chinese gang stormed out. The British boys put some money on the table and left a few minutes later. Steven returned to the table and sat down as if nothing had happened.

I've never seen such quiet authority, before or since.

There's only one more thing to tell of the time before Orion took over my life.

At 11 p.m. on a Thursday night, my water heater blew up, hurling pieces of metal around the bathroom and water all over the floor. I stood under my shower in shock, thinking of the FCC regulars who tried to trump one another with how scared they were of sudden sounds, and of what those sounds brought back for them. I didn't even bother to clean up. Instead, I turned off the water at the mains; dressed in clothes for the next day; and took a taxi to Jardine's Lookout, rehearsing on the way what I'd say.

But it was a stranger who opened the door. He had green eyes, wavy black hair, deep lines in his forehead and at the sides of his mouth. He was wearing a beige cotton robe that was too small. "I'm Adam Sarris," he said.

I was face-to-face with Steven's boss from London. Involuntarily, I ran my hand over the wet hair I hadn't bothered to comb. "I'm Laurie Michaels. My water heater blew up."

Adam laughed loudly and long, and I could see why the furrows on his face were so deep. He laughed with every muscle there was. "That's one of the unlikeliest things I've heard," he said. "Even Graham Danvers wouldn't have been able to match that." He took a few steps back, to let me in.

Steven came out of the bedroom with a towel around his waist. "What's all this about?"

"My water heater blew up."

He laughed. "You don't expect us to believe that!"

"It's true!"

Adam looked at Steven, at me, then at Steven again, and said: "I think I'll go back to sleep." He ambled to the guest room and closed the door.

chapter two

"Don't you dare suggest marriage to Steven," Graham Danvers
said. "If *he* capitulates, Adam will make it compulsory."

"Well now, Graham," Steven said, "if you got married,
you'd be able to buy another ring."

Graham, general manager for South-east Asia, wore so
many pieces of gold jewellery that Adam referred to him as
Fort Knox, to which Graham always replied: "No, school of
hard knocks."

"I've known Steve barely two months," I said.

Graham dismissed this with a wave of his hand. He, the
other Orion regional managers and their wives, saw me as
Steven's girlfriend and, therefore, as one of the gathering.

I looked around the table at La Plume, one of Hong Kong's
most expensive restaurants. Adam, managing director for the
Middle East, Asia and Australia, held court with anecdotes
that everyone had heard before but seemed happy enough to
hear again. Della Sarris sat beside her husband, long dark hair
piled on top of a slender oval face. Clockwise around the
table were Roger Benham, the Sydney-based general manager
for Australia and New Zealand, and his wife, Felicity; Dick
Staunton, Riyadh-based general manager for Saudi Arabia,
and his wife, Helen; and Christopher Kendall, general manager for the Gulf, based in Abu Dhabi, with his wife, Liz.
Graham Danvers sat next to Steve, general manager for
North-east Asia, who was sitting next to me.

The men were exuberant, clearly used to one another's

company. The women were chatty, too, but they did not share the same camaraderie, and so their liveliness was slightly forced, although not unpleasantly so. All of them had slim and long-legged frames clad in pastel-coloured suits. All of them had clear skin, clear eyes, posh English voices and the same mannerisms, as though they'd gone to the same finishing school – which, for all I knew, perhaps they had. My business-like navy blue suit suddenly seemed dowdy to me, and my accent gauche. I told myself to dismiss such thoughts.

But the next day, I spent lunchtime in Queen's Road, buying two suits, a silk dress, a silk scarf, shoes and a matching handbag. The credit-card tally was six and a half weeks' salary.

That evening, preparing for dinner at The Royal Garden, I looked in the mirror at my new beige suit, handbag and shoes. The outfit would have looked smashing on Della or Felicity, Helen or Liz, but on me it looked clumsy. It was something to do with the way I stood. What the hell, I thought – the four of them had been born into the British upper class; my grandparents had come from a *shtetl* in Lithuania. The best I could do was try to stand straight.

"Quite a change from the Middle East," Helen Staunton said. Liz Kendall laughed.

It was Sunday morning. We were walking through the narrow streets of Macau, having spent the night at the Pousada de Satiago. Washing flapped overhead on poles extended from windows. There were smells of food frying. And the clicketyclack, clicketyclack, clicketyclack of mah-jongg cubes was as persistent as cicadas.

"Riyadh!" sighed Helen.

"Come on," said Dick, "it's not that bad."

"Not for you," said Helen. "You're a man. You can go where you please."

I had listened eagerly all week to the casual comments made about expatriate life in the Middle East, trying to picture what life in Saudi Arabia must have been like for Steve. But Dick's Saudi Arabia was so different from what Steven had known as to be almost unrecognisable. "Except for the sand," Steve said.

"Lots of sand in Sydney, too," Roger Benham said. "Super beaches. Super city."

"I hate the place," said Felicity. "The only decent thing about it is the wine. It's not London. It's not Paris. It's not even Milan."

"At least it's not Singapore," Graham said.

"You *like* Singapore," Felicity said.

"True," said Graham. "I don't really mind where I am. So long as I'm making money."

"I don't mind, either," I said, "so long as it's somewhere else."

"Somewhere else?" asked Adam. "What do you mean?" But I could see he knew perfectly well what I meant. "Somewhere else," he said again.

I liked Adam. I liked Graham, Roger, Dick and Christopher too; and Della, Felicity, Helen and Liz, despite their impossible elegance. I liked the atmosphere that Orion people created around themselves. I liked the stories, which had attained the status of myths, told about Jonathan Grosvenor and Ted Jennings, who had founded Orion Management Systems in 1976. Jonathan and Ted were such good salesmen, Adam said, that in the early Seventies they had sold sand – *sand!* – to a Saudi prince to put around his swimming pool. "They weren't selling sand," Adam commented; "they were selling prestige.

You've always got to understand what it is you're really selling."

There were anecdotes, too, about Orion sales executives, support consultants and hardware engineers, all of whom appeared to treat the different parts of the world as suburbs of one big city which was theirs to carve up.

During one marathon session after dinner, Steven and Graham had argued about which of them would be responsible for business in Vietnam once foreign contractors were allowed in to develop the oil deposits already found there. Adam jokingly suggested they could divide the country in two – "It's been done before," he said – and Steven and Graham laughed politely, before resuming their territorial tussle.

I wondered what the former Vietnam correspondents would have said about that. I wondered what the Vietnamese themselves would have said. The FCC crowd rarely mentioned the Vietnamese, other than the interpreters or the bar girls, or the shadowy presence of the North Vietnamese – the enemy in the jungle, among villagers, underground. The Vietnamese were referred to as though they'd been extras in what essentially had been a Western drama of failure and pointlessness. The books and films about the war that were beginning to appear treated the Vietnamese the same way.

Orion's attitude to Asia wasn't much different. "You all talk as though the Vietnamese, the Koreans, the Indonesians, the Chinese, Japanese, and Filipinos are around to undertake projects using Orion Constellation, and that's all," I said.

Adam frowned. "What do you mean?"

"You bludgeon in as the white man who knows best. Do you ever say hello in Korean or Bahasa Indonesia? Do you dovetail into their etiquette or negotiating styles?"

"Are you always so blunt?" Adam asked.

"Do you object to bluntness generally, or when it comes from a woman?"

Steven covered his eyes with his hand. Graham grinned.

"Well," said Adam, "we seem to have cut through mere battle for sales patch and got down to the war of the sexes. You sound like a feminist."

"Of course I'm a feminist."

"But you're wearing a silk dress and high heels."

"I meant to ask you about that dress," Steven said.

"What's wrong with it?" I demanded.

"Nothing," said Steven. "It's very nice."

"It's smashing," said Adam.

I smiled. "Silk dresses don't have much to do with what we're talking about."

Adam smiled, too, and Steven looked relieved. "Seriously," said Adam, "you've got a point. It's going to take a while for us Brits to remember we're no longer running an empire. Hey, did I ever tell you about the time I met the Sultan of Brunei?"

In the bar of the Marco Polo Hotel, Singapore, I watched the Oriental waitresses glide among the tables in long, closely fitted brown dresses slit to the tops of their thighs. The waitresses were Chinese, Malay, some of them the striking combination of the Straits Born. An Indian woman wearing a red-and-gold sari was mixing drinks.

I sat in the semi-circular velvet chairs with Adam, Steven, Roger and Christopher, waiting for Dick and Graham to join us. Singapore in early February was hotter and more humid than Hong Kong at that time of year but, inside the hotel, the ambience was the same as it had been the last time I'd been with the people here. The group simply had reassembled somewhere else, although this time without wives. I was in

Singapore independently, to help out on a feature supplement for the Chinese New Year edition of *ABT*.

The Orion crowd had convened to discuss a package deal they had proposed to a large Korean construction company involved in projects throughout Asia, Australia and the Middle East.

Dick was upstairs in his room, talking on the phone to one of his sales executives in Jeddah. Graham was chatting up an exquisite Eurasian hostess at the other end of the bar. He had two new gold bracelets on his right wrist.

When Dick walked up the shallow steps from the lobby into the bar, Graham reluctantly broke away from the hostess, and the group was complete, ready for dinner.

"Well," said Adam, when we were settled at a table in the Brasserie La Rotonde, "we might as well begin." He nodded to me. "*You* might as well begin. It was your idea."

"I doubt it," I said, smiling.

Adam returned the smile. "You suggested doing the article for *Asian Business Today*."

"I rather imagine the idea may have been planted in my head."

"Really? By whom?"

I looked at Adam's creased yet immensely boyish face. "It's impossible to get the better of you," I said. "I won't even try. Let's start with some background, perhaps." I took out a notebook and pen.

Adam leaned forward, breathed deeply, and embarked on the story of Orion. He started with Jonathan and Ted, salesmen extraordinaires who, with the help of Max James, genius programmer, had set up Orion Management Systems and had ridden the hi-tech boom. Project planning had been a new discipline just coming into its own. Jonathan and Ted had recognised a gap in the market for a project management system that would combine hardware and software in the proverbial black box.

I'd heard a lot about Jonathan and Ted before, but not much about Max James. Max, said Adam, had had the ideas but not the computer equipment to try them out on. He had friends, though, who worked as programmers in companies which had bought the new mini-computers that were then the wonders of the industry. Friends gave him keys and identity cards to allow him access to their offices at night. Max had whole corporate computer departments to himself between 10 p.m. and 6 a.m. He got to know the security guards: Max knew about the importance of detail. He completed a draft of the software in less than a year, and called it Orion Constellation – nobody knew why. "Perhaps," said Adam, "it was because he always wanted to be a star."

Everyone around the table laughed, except Steven, who was cutting his steak with the intensity of a surgeon. Steven hadn't been keen on the idea of a story for ABT. "What is it about Steven and journalists?" Adam had asked.

I shrugged. The interview was going well enough, although my editor had been almost as dubious about the story as Steven had been. He'd given the go-ahead only after I'd suggested a quirky lead. Orion Constellation was being used on a hotel going up in Macau, I'd told him. Labourers were excavating the caissons by hand because they'd always done it that way and because it would have been difficult to transport the necessary equipment to Macau. Yet the whole project, including the excavation, was being co-ordinated by computer. "I suppose that's interesting enough," he'd replied. But Steven hadn't thought so. "We're trying to sell state-of-the-art computer systems here," he'd said, "and you want to talk about excavating by hand?"

Steven continued to attack his steak. I continued to ask

Adam questions. The dessert came, and coffee, and Adam's answers merged into anecdotes of his latest visits to clients or prospects. When the port arrived, I tried to rein Adam back in.

"How does Orion Constellation work?" I asked.

"It's very user-friendly," he said. "It doesn't take long to learn."

"Yes, but how does it work?"

"It lets you control the project, instead of letting the project control you."

"How does it work?"

"It uses critical path method."

"I know, but how does it *work?*"

Adam stared at me with the amazement of a schoolmaster challenged by a pupil. I stared back.

Steven said: "You don't need to know that. *We* don't need to know that. The techos take care of it. Prospects want to hear about how Orion Constellation can make their life easier, not about how it actually works. They'll have more than enough time to learn that after they buy it."

"OK, Adam," I said, "I'll move on to something else. How big does a project have to be before buying Orion Constellation becomes economically justified?"

Steven, Dick, Christopher, Roger and Graham put down their liqueurs. They looked at me, then turned to look at Adam.

"That's the wrong question," he said. "A company should look at how much money an Orion system can save them, not at how much it costs."

"You couldn't justify buying Orion Constellation if, for example, you're going to build one small house," I said.

"Of course not."

"So how big," I said politely, "is a project likely to be before buying Orion becomes worthwhile?"

"It depends."

"I need an estimate. Without it, the article will have a serious hole."

"Fill it with something else."

"Journalism doesn't work like that," I said, trying to keep a lid on my irritation. "When people like you read an article like this, there are things you want to know. An approximate minimum project value would be one of those things, wouldn't you agree?"

Steven pushed his chair away from the table. "I knew this would happen," he said, his voice deeper than usual.

"She has a point," Adam said. He looked at me and scratched the back of his head. "Can we talk about this tomorrow? I'd like to give it some thought."

"Fine," I said, putting my notebook away. Adam smiled. Everyone except Steven relaxed, and the customary after-dinner anecdotes began.

"The last time Dick was in Singapore for a meeting," Graham said, "he arrived a day late." The others laughed in anticipation. "He was coming from Houston," Graham continued. "He forgot about the dateline."

Dick grimaced, and the others waited for what appeared to be the established counter-anecdote. "In Cairo," he said, "Graham bought an antique gold ring. Bargain price, he said. Bragged about it for months. I made him have it valued. Was it antique? Was it even *gold*?"

Graham shifted uneasily in his chair, but only for effect. Steven wasn't listening. I cast my mind back over the evening and wondered what it was I'd done that had been so wrong.

*

I awoke next morning feeling stiff and thick-headed. The air-conditioning didn't seem to be working properly and it was impossible to open the windows. I had slept only fitfully. Steven had been cold and distant when we'd gone to bed. He had curled up on his side and gone straight to sleep.

I got out of bed but lost my balance.

"It's my foot," I said, trying to steady my left ankle. "No, it's my head. No, it's my foot."

Steven watched from the bed, his face crumpled in laughter. "That's one of the funniest things I've ever seen."

I stood there, my balance regained, and looked at the way Steven's usually immaculately blow-dried hair was sticking up on top and out at the sides. "I love you," I said.

Steven stopped laughing. "That's the first time either of us has said that."

"I know."

He got out of bed and went to the cupboard, his back to me. "They're big words."

"I know."

"I don't think I can say them."

"That's OK."

"I still haven't thawed out from Saudi Arabia. No, that's an excuse. Those words – I've never been able to say them. Probably the closest I've ever come to saying them has been with you, but . . ."

"But?"

"There's just something . . ."

"Missing?"

"I don't know. To be honest, I haven't had time to think about it. There's something brewing with Adam – I can't tell you what it is – and I've had to be careful not to screw up."

"Why can't you tell me?"

"Because it hasn't been decided yet."

"If you can't confide in me, what's the point?"

"The point of what?"

"Us."

Steven stared at the floor. "We're going to be late for breakfast."

"Oh, for heaven's sake." I went into the bathroom and turned the hot water on full. It was unlikely that the Marco Polo's hot water system would blow up but, if it did, I didn't care.

"Are you all right?" asked Adam.

"Sure," I said, a little too loudly.

We were having breakfast in the coffeeshop, on the terrace outside.

"When Laurie got out of bed this morning," Steven said, "she couldn't stand properly. She said: *It's my foot. No, it's my head. No, it's my foot.*"

The others laughed.

"Not a bad story, that," said Graham.

"Worth remembering," said Dick.

"Perhaps," said Adam, "Laurie has fallen head over heels in love?"

Steven froze. I think I looked stricken.

"It's a joke," said Adam. "Foot. Heels. Oh." He fussed with the menu and signalled to the waiter.

The coffee and croissants, bacon and eggs, yoghurt and fruit, were eaten largely in silence.

"I think I'd like a bit more time before I give you answers to the questions you asked last night," said Adam.

I nodded.

"It's important to get these things right."

I nodded again.

"In the meantime, we have a Korean deal to nut out," Adam said. "Seoul to Seoul discussions, you might say."

I laughed. Adam lowered his head, raised his eyebrows, and stared straight at me in an attempt to make amends. I smiled and shook my head in a gesture of never-mind.

During that day, and the next, I went about mechanically, helping with layouts, headlines, captions, and all the other myriad details that make up a magazine. I was relieved not to be doing any interviewing or writing. The sub-editing tasks were soothing for a change. It was satisfying to get to the end of the day and see a few more pages of order, everything neatly in its place and pleasing to the eye.

The Marco Polo gave me a sense of order, too. It was luxurious yet anonymous, comfortable yet transient. It made the politeness between Steven and myself easier to bear. We had little chance to talk much anyhow. At dinner, Adam presided, with Steven and the others sitting around like disciples.

"I don't like it when you're down," said Steven, while preparing for bed. "You're usually so vivacious."

"Vivacious? You tell me there's something missing in our relationship, and you expect me to be vivacious?"

Steven stared at me. "Is *that* what all this has been about! Look, I feel warmer to you than I've ever felt. I *am* thawing out. Can't you tell? Don't cry, Laurie, *please*!" He flailed his arms about before finally enclosing me in them.

Steven and I sat at a table outside on the terrace of the coffeeshop. It was the day before the Orion contingent was due to leave for Seoul.

"I can tell you now," he said. "Adam has asked me to take over responsibility for South-east Asia. This is where everything's happening. I'm really pleased about it."

"Well!" I said, almost knocking over a glass of mineral water as I leaned across the table to give him a hug. "I suppose that means Graham will be reporting to you from Singapore."

"Yes."

"He won't like that."

"No. He particularly won't like it because Adam wants me to *move* to Singapore. Derek Williams – you'll meet him – will come out from London to fill the slot in Hong Kong."

"I could come and live in Singapore, too," I said. I saw the muscles in Steven's neck tighten, and mine did too. I hadn't known I was going to say that. Leave Hong Kong? For fewer opportunities in Singapore? But what did I have to lose?

Steven disentangled his shoulders from my arms and stared at the wrought-iron table with its red-and-white checked cloth. "I don't feel ready for that," he said.

I turned my head slowly towards the exuberant tropical garden. Was there anything I could say that would make a difference?

"We'll still see each other, of course," he said. "I'll be in Hong Kong often. But I can't make a commitment right now. There's too much happening. Maybe I don't want to grow up. Maybe I'm Peter Pan."

He left next afternoon for Seoul.

I returned to Hong Kong. Everything was shut because of Chinese New Year. Even the FCC was closed. Everyone I knew was away. When I rang Susan at *The Age* in Melbourne, the chief of staff told me that Susan hadn't been in for weeks. There was still no response from Susan at home.

My parents didn't answer, either. The history department

secretary said that Dr Michaels and Dr Michaels were in Canberra at a conference on historical method. My brother and my sister were out. I didn't know who else to call.

On the day Steven was due back from Seoul, I stayed behind at the office, listlessly typing some notes. Every few minutes I glanced at my appointment diary, in which I'd pencilled in the time of Steven's flight.

The phone rang, and I tried to sound nonchalant when I said hello.

"I'm at the airport," he said. "I'll get a taxi and pick you up."

In Steven's mind, apparently, we were still together, questions of geography a minor inconvenience. Steven spent most of March in Taipei; I had assignments in Peking, Hangzhou and Shanghai. Communication links had not yet been restored between Taiwan and mainland China, so Steven and I left messages with each other's offices in Hong Kong and Singapore, to be forwarded to our respective hotels by telex.

When I returned to Hong Kong, there was a long telex from Adam answering most, although not all, of the questions I'd asked for the article. (He'd evaded citing a minimum project value.) There was a telex from Steven containing his new Singapore address, which I recognised – an apartment in a small development around the corner from the Marco Polo Hotel. Only Steven would choose a flat by its proximity to a coffeeshop. There was another, later, telex which said: "Puerto Azul weekend after next. Ticket will arrive your office. Meet you Manila airport Friday night." It was signed Peter Pan.

*

At Manila airport I gave Steven a copy of *ABT*, which had the Orion article inside. He grabbed it eagerly.

"Great, isn't it!" he said, after reading the piece three times.

"Not a bad reaction from someone who was against the idea."

"Who was against the idea?"

"*You* were."

"Bollocks."

I didn't know whether he was joking or not but, before I had had time to think about it, he said: "Hey! Why are we talking about work? This is our weekend off!"

We took the bus from the airport to Puerto Azul, a resort as vividly blue in sea and sky as the name made it sound.

In our small timber cabin, among trees on a hill a ten-minute walk from the beach, I unpacked and ran a bath.

"While you're doing that," he said, "I'll ring Adam."

"You said this was a weekend off!"

"As soon as I've spoken to Adam."

"You're impossible."

He lowered his head and raised his eyebrows in a way I'd seen before. It was the look Adam had given me at the Marco Polo to apologise for "head over heels in love".

I shook my head and smiled.

When I came out of the bathroom, with a towel around my hair, I heard Steven say: "But she's my girlfriend."

"What was that about?" I asked later.

"Sometimes," said Steven, frowning, "Adam is just . . ."

"Just what?"

"Just Adam."

The next morning, while waiting for breakfast to arrive, Steven rang the office in Sydney. He put down the phone, and I waited good-naturedly for him to make another call. When he didn't, I said: "Surely that's not all!"

Steven scratched the back of his head. "Adam's on a plane to Houston. Graham would be driving to Ponggol to go water-skiing. Riyadh and Abu Dhabi are asleep."

"How do you keep all these time zones in your head?"

Steven grinned. "Dick's always going on at me about that. You must have heard about the time he arrived late in Singapore by a day."

I nodded.

"He used to get times mixed up all over the place. Sometimes he'd ring Adam in the middle of the night."

"Adam rings *you* in the middle of the night."

"That's different. Adam can do what he likes. Anyway, Dick bought three watches – imitation Rolex, maybe they were real, who knows? – and put them on his arm, alongside the one he had already. The original watch was on Riyadh time. He set the others to London, Houston and Hong Kong. That would have been OK had they been twenty-four-hour digital jobs, but they weren't. So he had no way of knowing if it was 4 *p.m.* or 4 *a.m.* in London, 10 a.m. or p.m. in Houston, midnight or noon in Hong Kong. In the end, he gave the Rolexes away."

I did some quick calculations. "You got all the times right," I said.

"See? It's not hard. Ever thought of going into business?"

"I'm a journalist."

"You're a business journalist. You write about people making money. Other people. Wouldn't you like to make money yourself?"

"There's more to working than making money."

"Of course. It's not the money that's important. It's the *game*. Money's the scorecard."

I stared at him. "You sound as though you mean it."

"I do mean it."

"Then you don't understand me very well."

Steven looked at me sharply. "Is business beneath you? Is that what you're saying?"

"Of course not," I said, confused. Was it, in fact, what I meant? If so, how was writing about business any different?

"You'd be good," said Steven. "You should consider it."

The phone rang after we'd already gone to bed.

Steven answered it, then handed it to me.

"I want to offer you a contract," said Adam.

I sat up. "What sort of contract?"

"For three months. To talk to all the Orion clients in Asia."

"All of them? Aren't they, um, scattered? Remote?"

"Scattered *and* remote. We'd like to know why they bought Orion Constellation systems, what they're using them for, what they think about the support services we provide, and how we can improve them."

"Why?"

"To know what our customer base wants, and to give it to them."

"You want to know what your existing customer base wants? Why?"

"To know how best to sell the system to others."

"That sounds a bit more convincing," I said. Steven got up and went out on the balcony.

"A lot of our clients in Asia are difficult to talk to, as you know," Adam continued. "It's not just a matter of language barriers. Some of our sales and support bods from the UK, bless their souls, have been wandering around alienating people in a way you wouldn't believe. But of course you'd believe it — you *alerted* me to it."

He paused. "You seem to handle the region better. And you seem to be able to get people to tell you things they don't intend to. I answered all the questions for the article."

"Not quite all of them."

"Some questions are better left as questions."

I let that pass. "What would happen after the three months?"

"It depends on you and it depends on us."

"What sort of an answer is that?"

"An evasive one."

"Adam!"

"I don't know. Anything might happen."

"Who would I report to?"

"Me."

"Where would I be based?"

"I thought you might ask that. Singapore."

"What does Steven think about this?"

"He said: *But she's my girlfriend.*"

"What did *you* say?"

"That I can hire anybody I damn well please."

"Why do you want to hire *me*?"

"Because you're the most impossible woman I've ever met."

"I'll ring you back."

I joined Steven on the balcony and was startled by the voluptuous tropical night.

"Well?" I asked.

"It's your decision."

"Where would I live?"

"With me, I suppose."

"You said you didn't want that."

"It would only be for three months."

"Peter Pan."

Panic flitted across Steven's eyes. "*You* decide," he said. "If you come, maybe it will be good. Maybe I'll get over this fear . . ."

"I didn't ask Adam about money."

"He'll give you what you're earning now, plus expenses. The company pays for my flat." He bit his tongue. "For our flat."

"That's not a bad deal. I'd like to accept."

Steven took a deep breath. "That's settled, then. You'd better ring your new boss."

chapter three

"That's an awful lot of luggage," said the woman behind the Cathay Pacific counter at Kai Tak airport, a Brit about the same age as me.

"That's all I own, in those eight suitcases," I said. "I should have shipped them. I didn't have time."

"Are you moving to Singapore, then?"

I nodded.

"Business or personal?"

"Both, I guess."

"My flatmate's thinking of moving there." She tapped at her keyboard, looked at the screen and smiled. "We're not full upstairs. I'll upgrade you to business class. That will double your baggage allowance and cut back on the charge for excess."

"I really appreciate this," I said, handing her my ticket and my American Express card.

She put tags on the suitcases and I watched them teeter, one by one, along the conveyor belt and disappear.

In the upper deck of the Boeing 747-stretch, I took the latest copy of *ABT* from the magazine rack. From now on, I'd be just another reader. I had left the office for the last time the afternoon before.

Flipping through the magazine, I saw a long interview I'd done – the last one, in fact – with Cathay Pacific's new deputy managing director. "How does the question mark hanging over 1997 affect Cathay Pacific's long-range planning?" I had asked him.

"Cathay used to have five-year plans," he had replied. "We cut that back to three. Beyond years two and three, you're in dreamland. We're conscious of 1997, of course, but fourteen years is a long time, particularly in Hong Kong."

Even ten days was a long time in Hong Kong. I had given notice at *ABT* (using untaken holidays to make up the required time); sold the furniture I'd bought not long before; found someone to take over the lease on my flat; written articles started or promised; and said goodbye to friends – none of whom had been enthusiastic about my new job.

"You're becoming a flake," Olivia had said. Even Susan, who finally answered her phone in Melbourne, said: "What happened to your idealism, your commitment?" Before I'd had time to reply, she said, "I'm sorry – I've been going through a bad time", but would not elaborate. She said she'd ring back, but she never did, and she didn't answer when I telephoned again.

I looked at the copy of *ABT* in my hand. It was not a world-class magazine – "Not *Fortune* exactly," the editor had quipped when I'd joined, "more like *mis*fortune" – but it had been a part of who I was.

A wave of apprehension covered me like sweat.

"*Eight* suitcases?"

Steven looked at the two trolleys I had wheeled into the arrival hall at Changi. "*Business* class? Who said you could come business class?"

"Hi," I said, "I'm pleased to see *you*, too."

"I suppose I should start that again," he said, taking one of the trolleys and wheeling it towards the exit. "But we're trying to cut costs. Business class isn't necessary on a three-and-a-half-hour flight."

"For heaven's sake, Steven, I was upgraded. I'm exhausted. It near killed me to be able to make this flight."

"You should have taken a couple more days, then."

I stared at him. "You insisted Adam wanted me here today."

"Yes, well. Adam's been delayed a few days, in Saudi Arabia."

"Do you mind," I said, trying to smooth over my anger, "if I go to the flat, then, rather than the office? I'd like to unpack."

"That's fine by me," he said curtly.

I was lying on the bed when Steven came home from work. He bounded up the stairs and reached the bedroom midway through kicking an imaginary soccer ball. He stopped and stood still. "All these shoes!" he said.

"There's nowhere else to put them. *Your* shoes take up the space in the wardrobe."

"What about the cupboard downstairs?"

"Waterskis. Four pairs of climbing boots."

"Oh. I'd forgotten about those." He stood in the doorway, his shoulders drooping as if to say: What have I *done*?

"I know," I said. "Territory."

Steven looked at the offending shoes one more time, as though to render them invisible. "You're always so reasonable," he said at last. "Give us a hug."

He lifted his arms and, in the brief moment before I put my head on his shoulder, I looked at him as a stranger might, and I tried to look at myself that way, too. I loved this man enough, I realised, to see the despair it could create. The power he had over me by what he did and said and felt was immense. A voice in my head said: "You're here, and that's enough." I repeated it several times, turning it into a mantra of sorts, a narcotic, a cloud.

I woke to the sound of Steven's alarm. This had come to mean hotels to me, and so I was momentarily surprised to see not the usual bland beige walls, a mirror and a desk, but framed photographs of the Lake District in England, and all my shoes. Steven was sleeping, in his own flat. I was lying next to him, in *our* flat.

"Hey," I said gently.

He moved his shoulders slightly, and stretched out his chest.

"Hey," I said again.

He opened his eyes, focused slowly, smiled. I couldn't remember when he'd smiled like that, first thing in the morning.

"Hi, beautiful," he said. "How about a hug?"

I snuggled into him, and Steven closed his eyes. His eyelids, like the rest of him, were covered in freckles. I'd never noticed that before.

In the car, I juggled hairbrush, mascara and toast, while Steven drove down Grange Road. "No more time, gotta go," he'd said at quarter past eight, his voice much deeper than the "How about a hug?" of an hour before. I finished the toast, and put the hairbrush and mascara away. We were now in Havelock Road. Havelock Road became Upper Pickering Street, then Pickering Street, then Church Street. With road names like that, you'd be forgiven for not knowing you were in Asia.

But then Steven turned right, into Telok Ayer Street, and the wide avenues of central Singapore, with their mixtures of colonial structures and late twentieth-century glass, gave way to a rapidly disappearing older Singapore of meandering narrow streets with two-storey shophouses, their merchandise overflowing from the ground floor on to the footpath. Old men sat at tables outside, sipping tea. Above them were the ubiquitous poles jutting from windows, holding washing that would take forever to dry because the humidity was like soup.

Steven made a sharp turn into Boon Tat Street. This was Singapore in transition. Most of the shophouses in the street had already been demolished; there were office towers in various stages of completion going up in their wake. On elaborate bamboo scaffolding were the names of construction companies, most of them Korean. The site workers were mainly Korean, too.

"Lee Kuan Yew might as well stamp *Korean-made* over the whole of downtown," I said. Lee Kuan Yew was Singapore's long-serving Prime Minister.

"They're our potential clients, managing those sites," Steven said. "You'll be dealing with them soon enough, believe me."

He veered into his car space on the lower ground floor of the multi-storey building in Robinson Road that could have been anywhere in the world. With what seemed like one fluid movement, he turned off the ignition, grabbed his briefcase, and got out of the car. The early morning Steven had gone; Steven was now At Work.

The office was on the sixth floor. I followed Steven out of the lift and through two glass doors, ORION in silver on each. A Chinese woman in her late fifties was cleaning the kitchenette.

"Good morning, Auntie," Steven said.

The woman bowed.

"Good morning," I echoed, and Auntie bowed again, her

traditional loose-fitting black cotton trousers and buckle-up slippers in marked contrast to the ergonomic furniture, computer screens, and elaborate appointment diaries which Steven referred to as time organisers. No one else had arrived.

Most of the office was a large open-plan area, where the technical support consultants and administrative staff had their desks. Along one wall were small separate offices for the support manager and the sales executives. The offices had glass partitions, so the separation was aural rather than visual. The corner office, which Steven had appropriated from Graham, was the only section with real walls, the only place you couldn't be seen.

"Come in," said Steven, opening the heavy timber door.

I looked around. "You're kidding," I said.

"I know."

The room was decorated in black and gold. By the window facing Robinson Road was a black leather couch. The black coffee table had gold drink coasters on it, and some gold executive toys that had to do with trying to get balls into chutes or balanced on top of other balls. The desk was black, with a gold telephone, gold in- and out-trays, and a black-and-gold blotter.

"I know," Steven said again.

"Graham must have been devastated when you took the office."

"He'll get over it."

"Where does he sit now?"

"In the office next to the support manager. He shares it with one of the other sales execs."

"One of the other sales execs," I echoed. "I see. Where are you going to put me?"

"You can share with another sales exec, in the office next to Graham, if you like."

He looked at his watch. "The others should start arriving now. Graham and the other sales execs are on the road – which is where they should be – and most of the support consultants are with clients. Hugh Spurling, the support manager, is in Jakarta. He'll be back tomorrow." Steven leafed through some papers in his in-tray. "Hugh will probably be of more use to you than I can be. He's been out here a lot longer than I have. So has Graham. The hard part's going to be to get them to co-operate."

I laughed. "Graham and I get on well. He's a friend."

"You work with him now. That's different."

"Why?"

"It just is. Also, I should warn you that you might get some resistance from Hugh. But you'll bring him round. You always do."

"Resistance?"

"The Number One secretary has arrived." Steven walked through his door into the open-plan area, clearly expecting me to follow, which I did.

The Number One secretary presided over a desk which stood at the midpoint between the entrance and Steven's office. She looked to be in her early twenties, but could have been older, with striking Hokkien features framed by permed red hair. She was wearing a Chanel-style suit, a jade pendant, and several jade bangles.

"This is Sandy Chan," said Steven. "This is Laurie Michaels."

"Pleased to meet you," I said. "Thank you for arranging my flight."

"No problem," said Sandy. She started to say something else but seemed to choke on the words. Instead, she nodded, then nodded again.

"Are you all right?" asked Steven.

"Work permit," said Sandy, nodding yet again. "Pregnant. Must not be. Must not get."

Steven stared at her.

"Guarantee," said Sandy, still nodding. She opened the bottom drawer of her desk and took out an official-looking document which she handed to Steven. He read it and, his face devoid of expression, leaned over on the desk and signed it.

Sandy relaxed and recovered her power of speech. "No one is thinking badly of you, not at all," she said to me. "The law is for the Filipina maids and the Hong Kong Chinese. But your employer must sign for you, too."

This was going to make a great story to tell Susan. In the meantime, though, I was going to have to keep a straight face. There were so many subtexts in what Sandy had just said, it would take a while to sort through them.

"It's a very nice office," I said.

The Number Two, Three and Four secretaries arrived, then the Number One and Two bookkeepers, all of them Chinese. Their grooming and dress was a mixture of Western and Chinese, and they spoke English with Chinese syntax. Singlish appeared already to be an advanced dialect. The cadences were Chinese, too – the rise and fall of the tones. It was very compelling, and I could see that I'd have to be careful not to fall unconsciously into its patterns, because mimicry, I was sure, would be interpreted as insult.

The women were staring at me quite openly. I knew from similar experiences in Hong Kong that my figure was being appraised; my clothes and jewellery, priced. I was also, no doubt, being compared to the Orion wives. I tried to stand straighter.

The others walked to their desks and started preparing for the day's work. Steven showed me what would become my

desk, in one of the offices behind the glass wall. We passed a
daunting block of four-drawer filing cabinets.

"They're the client files," he said. "You might as well start
there."

Each client file was several inches thick. What on earth could
there be left for me to find out?

A brief inspection answered my question. Each file contained details of the Orion Constellation sale (which had, in
some cases, taken up to two years), then itemised cases of
hardware malfunctions and software bugs that had (largely)
been fixed.

There were mountains of letters and telexes, but most of
them dealt with the making and changing of appointments. I
found little about the purposes for which Orion Constellation
systems had been bought, the uses to which they'd been put,
and whether or not these were the same. There wasn't much,
either, about specific client projects.

When I told Steven this, after everyone else had gone
home, he said: "We know that. That's why Adam hired you."

"I'll let you get on with it, then," Steven said after he'd
introduced me to Hugh Spurling.

Hugh crossed his arms. He was a slim, athletic, handsome
man, with dark blond hair and a steady blue-eyed stare. He'd
been with Orion almost as long as Steven had, and had been
sent to Singapore two and a half years previously, long before
Orion had officially opened an office there. In those days,
Adam had handled the sales, commuting from London, and
Hugh had provided customer support. I knew this from the
files – which was just as well, because Hugh's body language
made it clear that he intended to tell me as little as possible.

"What are you going to be doing?" he asked.

"Profiles of clients," I said, trying to sound low-key. "The projects they're involved in. The applications they're running on Orion Constellation."

"We've been very busy the past couple of years," he said. "There hasn't been time to write things like that down. We carry it in our heads. We get on with the work. There's a lot of work to do."

"I can see that," I said.

"I doubt it." He paused. "I suppose you've also been told to ask clients if they have any complaints about service."

"That's not part of my brief," I said, surprised. "Adam didn't mention anything like that."

"Didn't he now," Hugh said. He uncrossed his arms, walked to his desk and sat down. I gathered that our discussion had ended.

Graham seemed no more pleased to see me than Hugh had been. He wouldn't look me in the eye when I went in to his office to say hello upon his return from Jakarta.

"Jobs for the girlfriends, I see," he said.

"Graham! You *know* me. We're friends."

"That was before."

"But I haven't changed."

"Your role has changed."

"No one seems to want me in the office at all," I said to Steven that night, over dinner at the Marco Polo coffeeshop.

"They'll get over it," he said. "In any case, your job isn't to be liked. Only women need to be liked all the time. If *I* continually worried about being liked, I'd never get anything done."

I turned to look at the garden. It was almost like a person

to me, this garden. Had I done the right thing, accepting Adam's offer?

Steven reached across the table and touched my hand. "It's not that bad, surely," he said. "I really *am* glad you're here, and I don't mean only in the office."

I looked at his boyish face, his Off Duty face. Some initial hostility was a small price to pay for being here, in Steven's world.

Two days later, I stapled my thumb. The stapler missed the paper and hit my nail instead. I winced, and saw Charlotte Weng, the Number Two secretary, standing in front of my desk with a memo. She covered her mouth and fled the room in a flurry of stifled giggles. That was *all* I needed, I thought glumly. Now I had been seen to lose face.

But the incident had a different effect. The women in the office became kinder to me after that, less disapproving and cold. The only explanation I could come up with was that I'd turned myself into an honorary man – someone who was absentminded and inept when it came to such things as typing letters, adding up expenses, making photocopies, or stapling reports. That was what the female administrative staff were for, in their opinion. As an honorary man, perhaps, rather than as another woman, I no longer intruded upon their domain. Even Auntie treated me with new respect.

"Another flying visit to take snapshots," Graham said. He, Steven and I were waiting outside the Marco Polo for Adam to arrive on the overnight flight from Jeddah.

"Snapshots," Graham repeated. "He flies around the world taking snapshots, not realising that snapshots make things stand still. After they're taken, the scene has already changed."

"Give it a break," Steven snapped.

When Adam arrived, he picked up his briefcase and opened the taxi door in the one movement, the way Steven did.

"Saudia Air!" he said. "No drinks! But it's the only way of getting here from Jeddah without changing planes. Good to see you in Singapore, Laurie. I'll check in quickly, drop my bags, and ride with you and Steven to the office."

He rushed to the reception desk. None of us had had the chance to say hello.

"Doesn't he ever get jetlag?" I asked.

"Never seen it," said Steven.

When we arrived at the office, just before lunch, Adam went into conference with Steven, and I headed back to the files, eager to get the pilot study underway.

Reading the files had been a crash course in how Adam and Steven operated – how they got their leads, how they researched their prospective clients, and how they angled their sales pitches.

Most sales had taken at least twelve months. One sale had taken five years. The first items in each file showed that Adam usually had made the first contact. After a batch of letters, telexes, memos and telephone notes, Steven's name would crop up. The more recent sales had been initiated by Steven or Graham and taken over by one of the newer sales execs.

The names of the companies and their locations were magical to me. They were not the Asia of tourist brochures but of economic development. This was Steven's Asia. It would become mine, too, after visiting what I had come to think of as the Places of the Files.

chapter four

Sentences would begin *When I was in*, as soon as Orion people got together, and I started talking the same way. *When I was in* Bintulu or Pulau Batam, Jakarta or Trengganu, Kobe or Baguio, denoted more than place. It was Orion shorthand for the oil refineries and LNG plants, the steel mills and electricity authorities, the manufacturing plants and fabrication yards; shorthand for the managers and engineers, and the Orion Constellation applications they were using; shorthand for the way we fitted in there, socially as well as professionally. The end of the working day was rarely the end of the day with clients. Most sites were too remote for that.

It's strange what sticks in your mind.

I remember old men and children sitting on dusty oil pipes along the unpaved road between Pekanbaru and Dumai, watching oil tankers and dogs.

I remember a young boy running towards me across the planks linking the houses on stilts above the Brunei and Kedayan rivers in Kampong Ayer, the water village of Bandar Seri Begawan. I had strayed to the village from the Sultan Omar Ali Saifuddin Mosque, still barefoot and wearing the black overgarment provided at the entrance. The boy had an urgent question to ask me. "Where is," he said in broken English, "your *shoes?*"

I remember driving a battered rent-a-car across the Brunei – Sarawak border, full of glee at being here, in Borneo, vivid to me since high school from Joseph Conrad novels. Borneo had been as remote as you could get, in Conrad's day. It still was, I thought. But then I turned on the car radio and heard a rock 'n' roll band from my home town singing: "I said, do you speak-ah my language? / He just smiled and gave me a Vegemite sandwich."

The band, Men At Work, was popular in Asia. Australians in general were popular in Asia, except during diplomatic scuffles with Indonesia. I felt at home in the region in a way the British who worked for Orion did not. I'd learned Asian history at school; I'd studied alongside Asian students at university; and, like most Australians my age, I'd grown up regarding Australia as part of Asia rather than as outpost of a rapidly diminishing empire.

We Australians referred to Asian countries by name or, collectively, as Asia. We didn't speak of the Far East, the way the Brits did. It *wasn't* the Far East, to an Australian, and it most certainly wasn't the Far East to the people who lived there.

Clients became friendlier when they heard my accent. I also believed it was an advantage, being a woman. Steven had been dubious about this. Many clients, Japanese and Korean in particular, would be reluctant to deal with me, he'd said. Adam had predicted the opposite, and he proved to be right. I was able to get appointments with senior project directors and division managers whom Orion sales execs and support staff had been trying to see for months.

(Steven wrote a memo to Adam which Adam showed me, but not until months afterwards. It said: "Laurie has acted as something of a catalyst. Clients have voiced feelings they haven't expressed before. This has given us an opportunity to reopen support contract, upgrade and other negotiations which had stalled." It meant a lot to me, that memo; I only wished I'd seen it at the time.)

Invariably, the appointments would be made for late morning or late afternoon, and the meetings would flow naturally into continued discussions over a meal, except that the tables would turn and I'd be the target for interview. Was I married? (I said no.) Why not? Was it usual for young Australian women to work away from home and travel by themselves? Didn't I miss my parents? Didn't I want a husband? Didn't I want children? Didn't I want to be a *normal woman*? I smiled much, and gave noncommittal answers.

One time, though, very late at night, I sat with Jun Chung Kuy, the project director of a worksite in Sumatra, with senior managers even more delighted than I was to have been invited for coffee in Mr Jun's living quarters.

The lounge had a panoramic view of the refinery. Outlined by moonlight, the pipes and machinery looked like an artist's impression of Mars. (*When I was in Mr Jun's lounge room*, I would begin my description, back in the Singapore office.)

"You would make a good temporary wife," said Kim Han Ik.

I stared at him, then at his colleagues, all of whom were grinning broadly, their cheeks and eyes glowing from the *soju* we had drunk with our meal of *kimchi* and rice in the managers' dining room.

I had spent an exhausting two days interviewing these men. I had nodded attentively during explanations of mechanical components and chemical processes. I had sung Waltzing Matilda and Advance Australia Fair on request. I'd even fielded questions about the apparently legendary virility of Bob Hawke, Australia's newly elected Prime Minister. Now, over coffee and more *soju*, in this, my farewell, I was being told I'd make a good temporary wife.

"Is a compliment," said Mr Kim.

"Temporary wives are usual on site," said Lee Young Min, who had studied in the United States.

"Does everyone have one?" I asked.

"Of course," said Mr Lee. "Senior engineers and managers have several wives. You have as many temporary wives as you can afford. They are not prostitutes, you must understand, they are wives – temporary ones. They cook for us and mend our clothes. And do a few other things." The rest of the group laughed. Mr Kim glared at them, before turning back to me. "We look after them. They are honorable, we are honorable."

Mr Kim had had enough Western experience, I decided, for me to look at him directly and say: "That sounds perfectly reasonable to me. Back home, do your wives have temporary husbands?"

The expression on Mr Lee's face showed me that I had misjudged, but it was too late to retract.

The men sat in stunned silence for almost a minute, then started talking together in rapid Korean.

"That is not a sensible suggestion," said Mr Lee finally. "Women don't have such needs." He paused. "Do Western women. Do *you*?"

"Of course women do," I said.

There was the same stunned silence as before.

"We have heard about women's liberation," said Mr Jun. "Please would you explain what it is?"

I couldn't believe it. We had reached beyond work, beyond politeness, beyond cultural boundaries. We were talking, really talking, without overlay. "Women believe we have the right to make choices," I said. "We believe we have the same right to work as men do, and to be independent if we want to."

There was much discussion in Korean before Mr Jun said: "That may be all right for a few women, but only a few. Otherwise the world would fall apart."

I did not let my disappointment show. Instead, I smiled at

Mr Jun out of recognition for the skilful way in which he'd brought the discussion to a close, allowing everyone to save face. There were several more toasts – to me, to Orion, to Korea, to Australia, and to Orion again, for bringing us together. The evening ended with much goodwill.

But that night I lay awake in the hard narrow bed in the timber huts which housed Indonesian women who worked as cleaners (the concrete Korean engineers' barracks had been deemed unsuitable because of the shared showers). I thought about the young Korean women I'd met who worked as "office ladies", some of them with university degrees, making photocopies and tea. How could they bear it? How long would things take to change?

Steven's response when I mentioned all this later was: "You're in business, not women's liberation. You're not on a personal crusade. What you have is a job."

I didn't reply. I never got the last word, where Steven was concerned. But the feminist revolution did, indeed, arrive in Asia, at the end of the Eighties. Japan led the way. Office ladies got themselves on to the *sogo shoku* – the career track – at last, and a new term was coined: *oyaji-gal*, a single, independent, working girl who knew what she wanted and would not be deterred. I liked to think of myself that way, of course. How wrong I was; what a long way I had to go.

Between trips to the Places of the Files, I wrote up interviews and arranged subsequent visits, talking to the Orion staff involved. Everyone was enthusiastic and helpful, except Hugh, who stared at the floor. He spoke in monosyllables; his frown could fill an entire room.

I gave him copies of my reports anyway. Other copies went to Steven and, of course, to Adam. I culled relevant information into separate Client Profiles – for general use in the office – and started a Quotable Quotes file for sales execs to use with prospects, and for use in promotional literature and advertisements.

Steven was particularly pleased with the profiles and the quotes. Adam must have been, too, because he sent them to Jonathan Grosvenor in Houston, although I didn't find that out until I got a memo from Jonathan saying that he'd be in Singapore at the end of September, and that he'd like to hear more about the client survey then.

"Why is Jonathan coming to Singapore?" I asked Steven.

"How did you know that?"

"I got a memo from him."

"You got a memo from *Jonathan*?"

I showed it to him.

"It's *hand-written*," he said.

Later that evening, during Steven's customary chat on the phone with Adam, downstairs in the middle of the night, I heard Steven say: "It was hand-written, I swear it."

Adam renewed my contract until the end of the year, to extend the survey to clients who had bought Orion Constellation in the preceding three months. I was ecstatic: I was part of Orion now and, at the very least, was Steven's temporary wife. Steven hummed in the shower when we were together in Singapore. When we were apart, we talked on the phone from hotels all over Asia, in a telegram-like language that was uniquely ours.

"Waking up alone is so *boring*," he said once. It was the closest he had come to a declaration of love.

The night before Jonathan and the others were due to arrive,

Steven suggested to Hugh that the three of us have dinner. "Why?" Hugh asked suspiciously, although he couldn't very well refuse.

In the Hilton coffeeshop, Hugh glanced at Steven several times while the two of them were supposed to be concentrating on the wine list. Steven pretended not to notice.

The waiters took our orders, and the three of us sat in silence. Steven was usually adept at keeping talk flowing during meals with colleagues and clients, but that night he appeared to be making no effort at all. Hugh, normally taciturn anyway, was clearly on guard.

When the meals arrived, I turned to Hugh and said: "I believe you joined the company just before Steven did."

"Yes."

I waited for him to continue, but he didn't.

"What did you do before that?" I asked.

Hugh stopped eating and, for the first time since I'd known him, looked directly at me. "That's none of your business," he said.

Only then did Steven say anything. "Did you see how abominably Arsenal played last week?" he asked.

"Yes," Hugh said. The two of them talked about soccer games thousands of miles away for the rest of the meal, but the estrangement between them had intensified.

On the way home, after we had dropped Hugh at the office to pick up his car, Steven said: "What do you think of him?"

I wasn't sure how I should reply. Whenever I'd been critical of Steven's colleagues in the past, he had defended them. Good managers always dwelt on the positive, he said.

"I find him difficult," I said.

"He is, isn't he? He doesn't have the right attitude. He doesn't fit."

"He gets the job done, though," I said quickly, perhaps to

show that I understood it wasn't necessary to like people to be able to work with them.

"I'm not so sure," said Steven. He was staring at the road. "You've mentioned that some of our clients have complained about the time it takes Hugh to get back to them."

"Some of those complaints are unreasonable."

"I'd like you to write a report for me on what was said."

"Why?"

"Because I want you to. But I want it just for me. No copies."

"I'll do it tomorrow."

"I'd appreciate it. You don't need to mention it to Graham or anyone else."

"If you say so."

"Well," he said, his voice and face becoming bouncier, "at least the Hilton didn't let us down with the food!"

"No."

At last, he looked at me. "You seem tired," he said.

"Yes." But it was more than that. Something important had happened that evening, I wasn't sure what or why. I had unwittingly played out a role assigned me, without knowing what it was or what it had been designed to achieve. It would be years before I'd understand what had happened that evening, and years more before I'd stop feeling guilty about Hugh and angry at Adam and Steve.

I slept badly that night. The relentless whirring of the air-conditioner entered my dreams in the form of tanks invading a country I couldn't recognise, except for one long, wide, straight thoroughfare that looked much like the road to Changi airport.

The dream came back to me while driving along the road

the next day to meet Adam's flight. Steven was at the office making last-minute preparations for Jonathan, who would arrive that evening from Houston with Ogden Burroughs, Orion's financial controller. The regional managers would arrive during the afternoon. I was pleased to be going to pick up Adam alone. The drive to the hotel would probably be the longest unbroken amount of time I'd have with him during the visit.

Adam seemed unusually subdued when he walked into the arrival hall with his briefcase and suit-carrier. He looked crumpled and tense.

"Are you all right?" I asked.

"Della's talking of leaving me," he said.

"That's terrible," I said. Adam always got to the point so *quickly*.

He nodded. "I don't understand it. My feelings for her haven't changed."

"You're never there to *show* your feelings," I said. "Perhaps Della's trying to get your attention, to change how you live."

Adam sighed. "You're probably right. But I don't want to change how I live. And I don't think Steven wants to change how he lives, either. I think you should know that. Do you mind if I have a nap in the car on the way to the hotel?"

I drove to the Marco Polo along the road that had loomed so menacingly in my dreams the night before, with Adam uncharacteristically slumped in the next seat. He perked up when we arrived, and asked me to wait while he had a shower. I had a snack in the coffeeshop. During the drive to the office, he chatted about work. He didn't mention Della again.

At the office, the secretaries were all wearing new dresses. The men had slicked back their hair and polished their shoes. There were flowers on desks and in the kitchen. Sandy Chan stood at her desk – her commanding post – and surveyed the scene.

The highlight of Sandy's preparations for the visit was a dinner in a private dining room at the Mandarin Hotel. Sandy had ordered a banquet of duck, eel, pigeon and trout. Jonathan reigned over the gathering like an emperor. Ogden Burroughs sat on his right. Ogden had not been to Asia before and was having difficulty using chopsticks. Adam sat on Jonathan's left. Although not as subdued as he'd been at the airport that morning, Adam seemed less ebullient than usual, less *Adam*. It occurred to me that Jonathan was, indeed, the emperor here. Adam was a courtier. I'd never seen Adam in a subordinate role before. Steven, too, was less Steven than usual, toning down his personality appropriate to his position in the third tier. Christopher Kendall, Dick Staunton, Roger Benham, and Derek Williams – who had recently taken over Orion Hong Kong – also behaved in a suitably subdued way. Only Graham seemed aggressive, if just in small ways.

I watched as dishes were passed around, along with Orion anecdotes from different regions. The office staff deferred to the support consultants and sales execs, who deferred to Steven. Steven deferred to Adam, and Adam deferred to Jonathan. How was I behaving? I was watching. Where did I fit in? I didn't. I wasn't in the hierarchy – I was an offshoot, a satellite of Adam and Steve. Whatever little power or authority I had, I had as a result of being associated with them. On my own, I had no authority at all.

These thoughts hit me with great clarity. I'd always been an observer by inclination. In going into journalism, I'd become an observer by profession. Three months before, without thinking much about it, I'd left that profession, although admittedly for an assignment in which I'd be using journalistic skills. I hadn't realised how different my new role would make me feel. Newspapers and magazines generated information for its own sake; journalists were key players. Corporations like Orion generated information in order to use it and make sales. The people who mattered most were those who acted on information, not those who gathered it. As the person conducting the customer survey, I was an adjunct – a useful adjunct, perhaps, but an adjunct nevertheless. I didn't like that. I'd always been happy before, watching from the sidelines. What had changed?

This had changed: When I gave the presentation on the customer survey to Jonathan, Adam and Steven the next morning in the office conference room, I felt intoxicated with the energy these three men focused on me. Jonathan had been Adam's mentor; Adam had been Steven's mentor; and I realised that I had started to see myself as being apprenticed to Steven.

But when I finished the presentation, Jonathan said, "You've done excellent work, it will be put to good use," and I felt insulted. Jonathan had meant to compliment me but, in doing so, had underscored what I'd been thinking the night before – about the line between information-gatherers and decision-makers. Jonathan got up from the table, walked me to the door, and patted me on the shoulder. As I walked into the corridor, the door swung shut.

Steven didn't come home until well after midnight. The door to the conference room had remained closed all afternoon and into the evening. At nine o'clock, I had gone home.

When Steven saw that I was awake, he twirled around several times and let out a high-pitched squeal.

"You sound like a banshee," I said.

Steven did it again.

I laughed. "You're drunk."

"Jonathan promoted me!"

"Where to?"

"Here."

"You're already here."

"He gave me all of Asia! Managing director for all of Asia! Not just the South-east, but the North-east too!" He started taking off his clothes piece by piece and flinging them around the room. This was an amazing spectacle: Steven was usually so neat.

"You're *very* drunk!" I said.

"I'm the king!" he said, walking unsteadily towards the bed, wearing one blue sock. "Yes, I'm the king." He looked around the room. "I don't like this castle any more. I'll get another one."

With that, he got into bed, chuckled to himself, and fell asleep.

I lay awake and thought about how rapidly everything was happening. The manic expansion of the Eighties is legendary now, of course, as is embarrassment about its naivety and greed. But, in the early years of that decade, anything seemed possible if you pinpointed a need and worked shrewdly to fill it.

Effective project management was one such need, especially in Asia and the Middle East, where newfound prosperity was being channelled into large-scale development.

Adam, Steven, Graham and Orion's other sales executives kept up with who was planning to build what where. They researched the companies and the projects planned, and drew up proposals showing how computer project management in general and Orion Constellation in particular could help track projects, bringing them in on budget and on time. They targeted key executives in prospective client companies and stalked them with charm, during presentations and phone calls, over dinner and games of squash.

Steven was sharper than Graham and the others. He could see more clearly and more quickly which companies would be likely to buy. And he had learned from Adam that decisions were not always made by those whose job it was, that there was always a behind-the-scenes network of influencers. Steven would find those influencers and ally himself with them, help them sell the system to their own bosses. His energy and persistence were remarkable. So was his resilience. He was like a skittle in a bowling alley. "Knock me over," he'd say with a grin. "I'll bounce right up again."

Jonathan, Ogden, Adam, Christopher, Dick, Roger and Derek left, and the hunt for a better castle began. Five estate agents were engaged to find the perfect flat.

"What I want," Steven explained one evening to a bewildered young man who'd already shown us half a dozen impressive flats, "is something where the living room is spacious but cosy, the dining room separate but not enclosed, views from all main rooms, and a central location that isn't on a main road. That's what I want."

He repeated the requirements, with a profusion of "I wants". Perhaps I imagined it, but the agent looked at me scornfully, as if to say: If the flat's for him, then who are you?

Steven never used "we", unless referring to Orion. If Graham asked us to go waterskiing, for example, or to a party, Steven would say, "I'll try to come." Each time he said this, I thought about making a joke of it, so that he might say "we". But I didn't. It seemed too significant to mention.

My life consisted of Steven, Orion, and Singapore, all of which were inextricably bound. I had nothing outside of that.

Those three things weren't really mine, I realised, anyway. In Singapore, I was a foreigner, my residence permit dependent on the job. In Orion, I was a consultant working on the periphery, however much access I might have to the centre. And Steven? Steven talked of *his* flat, *his* career, *his* future.

"What am I going to do?" he asked one night after we'd come home from seeing yet another flat that didn't measure up. "I've got all these problems at work, and I can't seem to find a reasonable flat."

I put my handbag on a bench in the kitchen and turned to face him full-on. "*You've* got problems at work!" I said. "*You* can't find a flat. What about *me*? I'm here, too."

Steven looked at me in surprise. "But your contract finishes at the end of the year."

He was right, of course. We hadn't talked about it, but I had assumed without thinking too much about it that I'd stay on, in the new flat, working for Orion or perhaps getting a job on a magazine.

My mouth felt very dry. I got myself a glass from the cupboard and some mineral water from the fridge.

"I want to stay here with you," I said quietly.

Steven looked at the floor. "I'm not sure about that," he said. "We've had a wonderful time and all that but – well, you know me! – I haven't thought beyond that."

"Maybe the time has come to try."

He didn't look up.

"The point is," I said, "what do you feel?"

"I don't know."

"You must know what you *feel*!"

"Peter Pan," he said. "It's not a joke. I mean it. I really don't know what I feel."

"This Peter Pan excuse is wearing thin," I said. "One day

you're going to have to make up your mind. One day you're going to have to decide just what it is you do or do not feel. *Look at me!*"

He didn't.

I threw the glass I was holding against the wall, where it smashed and fell in splinters to the floor. I stood there paralysed with dread. A heat rash started on my neck and spread down my arms. I couldn't breathe properly.

Steven started sweeping up the pieces. I reached for another glass and smashed that against the wall. Steven started sweeping up those pieces, too.

"Don't you react to *anything*?" I screamed, throwing three more glasses in succession.

Steven ducked, and I ran out of the flat.

When I got downstairs, I thought: But where can I go? The Marco Polo coffeeshop? What was the point? In any case, I didn't have my purse with me. Neither did I have car keys. It was far too hot to walk around outside, and I couldn't stay in the car park without inviting speculation from the other inhabitants in the block.

I went back upstairs. Steven was sitting at the dining-room table, his briefcase open beside him. He was shuffling memos, his face down. When he looked up, his eyes were red, the skin around them white.

He pushed back the chair, stood, walked towards me and drew me to him. "I know you'd like me to be affectionate and say 'I love you'," he said. "It wouldn't be natural for me and I don't intend to do it. But I do like having you here, and I do want you to stay, at least in the short term. Who can know, anyway, what the long term holds?"

I was too upset to speak.

"Let me tell you what I was thinking, before you started throwing glasses," he said, trying to smile. It looked more like a grimace. "There's so much going on at work. I've hired Lucy and Ian Phillips from London. They'll be coming out next month."

I tried to speak normally, to *be* normal. Talking about work was a good place to start. Steven had mentioned Lucy Phillips before. She was a former schoolteacher whom Orion had hired in its early days to teach clients how to use Orion Constellation. As sales had increased, new trainers had been hired, and Lucy had become training manager. "Will she be training clients or trainers?" I asked.

"A bit of both," said Steven. "She'll be dynamite out here. The Japanese and Koreans will love her. They seem to like working with Western women."

I smiled; was about to say "But you said . . .", then changed my mind.

"What will Ian be doing?"

"Software support." Steven hesitated. "That's what I hired him for. But there are complications. I have to fire Hugh Spurling tomorrow."

"Why?"

"He has to go."

"Why?"

"I'm too tired to explain."

So the unease I'd felt over that night at the Hilton with Steven and Hugh had been justified. But I was tired, too – too tired to try to persuade Steven to explain. Steven was a master of persuasion and a master at resisting it. Only Adam and Jonathan had any authority over him. I felt the way I had as a child: small and insignificant, at the mercy of powers beyond sway.

The next day was hotter, more oppressive than usual. The

heat seemed to defy the air-conditioning system and seep into the office. Sandy Chan filed her nails. The Number One and Two bookkeepers appeared to make their ledger entries in slow motion. The whole room was bathed in fatigue.

For me, there was also a sense of foreboding. Hugh, unaware of what the morning held in store, talked to one of the hardware engineers about a problem in Bintulu. "You'd better go there tomorrow," he said. "They're threatening not to renew the support contract next month."

The engineer nodded.

Steven called Hugh into his office just before lunch. Hugh gathered that month's worksheets and walked into the corner office briskly, normally.

Fifteen minutes later, Hugh emerged from the office with his head down, his shoulders slumped. He passed by my office on the way to his own. A few minutes later, he passed by again, carrying jacket and briefcase.

The whole office watched, speechless, as he left the office without saying goodbye to Sandy Chan. Orion staff left the office hurriedly for one reason or another all the time, but never without saying goodbye to Sandy Chan.

I felt faint. I hadn't caused this, of course, but I'd been used to help bring it about. Why? I didn't like Hugh, but he hadn't done anything other than his best, given the difficulties of servicing the region with insufficient staff. Hugh didn't fit in, Steven had said. Was that grounds for firing someone? Or was there something else?

After Hugh had gone, the glass doors with the silver ORION logo still swinging behind him, everyone in the office froze a few moments before pretending to resume work. I pretended, too, but all I could think of was that I'd just seen a preview of how it would be for me. Only I wouldn't be fired from the company; I'd be fired from Steven's life.

Hugh did not turn up for work after that. He collected some personal items at the weekend, and that was that. But there was a postscript. It came in the form of a telephone call at 2 a.m.

Steven's voice was sleepy when he answered the phone, but his tone became sharp and alert almost immediately. "Hugh," he said, "it's the middle of the night."

"I don't see why you should sleep soundly, you bastard." Hugh must have been screaming into the phone; I could hear every word.

"This isn't necessary," Steven said.

"I know what you're up to." The words were loud and slurred.

"You're drunk."

"Firing me is your right. I won't contest that. But I *will* contest giving up my shares. You've changed the rules. You're swindling me."

"Now look here," said Steven. "I didn't make the rules, as well you know, and I didn't change them. You'll be paid for the shares, and for the remainder of your contract, and you have the flat and the car until the end of next month. It's a generous arrangement. I'm going back to sleep. Good night." He put down the phone.

"What shares?" I asked quietly.

Had Steven been properly awake, he would have told me that this was outside what I needed to know. But he answered without thinking. "When Jonathan was here," he said, "he drafted a legal document to the effect that only people working in Orion can own shares. If you leave, you have to sell the shares back to the company. It's a way of keeping control in the company."

Steven slid back into sleep. I lay awake for a long time. It was becoming a habit, not being able to sleep. I was going to have to do something about it.

Hugh left Singapore not long after that. He went to Jakarta, where he set himself up as an independent applications consultant for companies which used Orion Constellation systems. He was the most experienced Orion applications consultant in Asia, and he was inundated with work. He didn't even have to undercut Orion's standard consulting rate. He started earning four or five times his Orion salary and looked set to deprive Orion of a significant part of its application consultancy.

Steven was furious. I kept my thoughts to myself. I wished it were possible for me to tell Hugh how pleased I was for him.

chapter five

Lucy Phillips had a face like a pale exotic moon. It was creamy
skinned and almost perfectly round, with large blue eyes and
a plump pink mouth. She wore her blonde hair in a fringe to
her eyebrows and shaped along the line of her jaw. Her breasts
and hips were heavy and round, too.

Lucy's looks would have been noteworthy in any setting,
but in Asia they were extraordinary. I was almost as fascinated
by her as were Sandy, Charlotte, and the other women in the
office. It was a relief to be out of the spotlight, to be taken
for granted. If Lucy was perturbed by the stares, she didn't
show it. Lucy was devoid of self-consciousness, it seemed to
me.

Ian didn't have the same self-assurance. He was six foot
two at least, possibly six foot three. Like Lucy, he was pale
and blond, but his body was as thin and angular as hers was
curved. When he stood in the doorway of his new office,
previously Hugh's, he shifted his weight from one long leg to
the other and his arms dangled awkwardly at his sides. His
head was wide and flat on top, narrowing towards the chin,
approximating a triangle. When he blinked his grey-blue eyes,
he looked like a startled moose.

"I'd forgotten you were so *tall*," Steven said to Ian in the
Brasserie at the Marco Polo, where Lucy and Ian would stay
until they found a flat. Lucy and I laughed.

"Steven's been in Asia so long," I said, "he's forgotten he's
actually short."

"You're going to have a hell of a time in Japan," Steven said to Ian. "You'll have to bow from your knees. You're in for a shock!"

"I've had a shock already," Ian said. "I came out here expecting to work for Hugh Spurling. I arrive and find I've got his job."

"Here's to your promotion," Steven said, raising a glass of wine.

"Seconded," I said.

"To you, sweetheart," said Lucy, raising her glass as well.

"I don't know if I've had enough experience," Ian said. "I don't know if I can do it."

"Of course you can," said Lucy. "Anyway, I'm here to help you."

Ian swallowed and blinked.

Later that evening, when Steven and I were preparing for bed, I commented on Ian's anxiety and asked Steven if he thought Ian would be able to handle the job.

"He's twenty-seven years old," said Steven. "It's sink or swim. Orion's like that. *Life's* like that."

"Rough seas out here," I said, putting away my shoes in a cupboard I'd bought for them.

"He's got a life-jacket," said Steven, hanging up his suit.

"Lucy?"

"Yes."

"Do you think that's fair?"

"I wanted to hire *her*, and he came as part of the package. Do you think *that's* fair?" Steven got into bed. "As things have turned out, it might be for the best. But he's damned lucky. He wouldn't normally have got such an opportunity." He paused. "Well," he said gently, "are you coming to bed or not?"

I turned around from fussing with my clothes and stood there uncertainly, almost shy. On Steven's face was a welcoming, ardent look I hadn't seen for quite some time.

"Sweetheart," I said, realising only after I'd said it that I was using Lucy's endearment rather than one of my own.

Lucy had been hired as a trainer, but the first thing she did was reorganise the office. This involved streamlining the filing system and moving furniture around to create a space cordoned off by screens, for demonstrations and training sessions.

I wondered if Steven would object, but what he said was: "Lucy can really get things into shape, don't you think? I'm glad she's here."

I was glad she was there, too. She reorganised where the sales executives sat and moved in to share with me. Pot plants appeared, two photographs of Lucy's niece, and a tapestry that Lucy had made herself, which she draped over the back of her chair. The final touch was a small aquarium, which sat on a stand by the window, next to my desk.

Lucy had been with Orion five years. Her knowledge of Orion Constellation was extensive, and she answered questions briskly, confidently, like the former schoolteacher she was. She also had a brisk, confident way of asking questions. "I haven't been in Asia before," she said. "There are heaps of things I need to know."

I told Lucy everything I could think of, and gave her copies of the client profiles and survey reports I'd written so far.

"No one's done anything like this in Orion before," she said.

*

The flat in Farrer Road had richly textured tapestries on whitewashed walls, and rugs on polished timber floors. There were pot plants and holiday snaps, and a large collection of Lladro porcelain figurines.

I gave Lucy the fruit bowl I'd bought as a housewarming gift. Ian asked if Steven would like a beer.

"Sure thing," he said, picking up one of the figurines and turning it over in his hand before putting it carefully back in its place on a small table at the side of a deeply cushioned couch.

I watched him with a sudden surge of inadequacy. I'd always prided myself on being a career woman; I'd always regarded myself, I suppose, as being "above" domestic things. Here I stood, watching Steven linger on a figurine.

"I prepared things a bit early, perhaps," Lucy said, "but are we ready to eat?"

"Definitely," said Steven. "The smells from the kitchen knocked me out the minute I walked in."

Lucy smiled and busied herself in the kitchen, returning with a platter of roast lamb and potatoes. She put the platter on a cork mat in the centre of the table. Everyone sat down except Ian, who remained standing in order to carve.

"I can't remember the last time I had a meal like this," Steven said. "Restaurant meals aren't the same."

"It looks terrific," I said, too loudly.

Steven had two helpings. He had two helpings of Lucy's excellent trifle, too.

"What about the flat in Cairnhill Road we saw last week?"

"No," said Steven. "We'll stay here. I'll renew the lease."

"But you don't like this flat."

He turned away. "It's just a place to sleep."

I looked around the flat, which was almost as anonymous as the hotel rooms where we'd got to know each other. It symbolised everything that was wrong with our relationship. But relationships, for Steven, were not things you analysed or weighed. They happened or they didn't. In any case, they were peripheral. Work was where the important battles were won and lost, where the territory of self was mapped.

The only way to build a relationship with a man like Steven was to live in the present and let the present accumulate into a past which would, without his even noticing, turn into a future. I decided to take more of an overview with Orion, come up with some good ideas. Steven would see them; Steven would see *me*.

Good ideas are usually the simplest; they make themselves known when you've cleared your desk and shut the door. (I learned that from Jerry Sokolov in Hong Kong.)

Hugh Spurling had lost his job. I still felt uneasy about it. Many of the customer complaints about him, as I'd pointed out to Steven, had been unreasonable. They'd come largely from Korean customers who had understood only part of their Orion training because of limited English which they'd been too ashamed to admit. Why not train these engineers again? Not a refresher course – that would involve loss of face – but an "advanced seminar". For valued customers, at Orion's expense.

Lucy ran the first advanced seminar in November, for Korean planning engineers from sites throughout Asia. Most of the engineers had been using the system only for critical path planning and job cards. They went back as heroes, able to do cost breakdowns and "what if" projections. Orion support consultants heard from them less often and were able to get on with other things.

The savings in terms of time, telephone calls and travel costs were significant. Here were results – real results – that affected the bottom line. Steven told everyone how successful the seminars had been, and how well Lucy had conducted them.

To her credit, Lucy said: "They were Laurie's idea."

"Of course," said Steven. "I almost forgot."

Advanced seminars became a staple of Orion training in South-east Asia and, later, in South America. The other "good idea" for which I can claim credit came about by accident. ("Often the case," Jerry Sokolov would have said.)

"I always get the logo on crooked," a planning engineer muttered in Pulau Bukom over coffee one night after our interview for the client survey officially had ended. I looked at the logo – a rubber stamp, crooked indeed – in the right-hand corner of the report. The report contained four-colour bar charts of construction progress, pie graphs of cost breakdowns, and other state-of-the-art graphics that Orion Constellation could do.

"It's crazy that logos should be affixed with rubber stamps," I told Steven when I returned to Singapore.

He looked thoughtful. Next day, he offered a bonus to the support consultant who could write a program for the logo. Simon Tan did it in two days and installed it a week later. The engineer bought him dinner and gave him a printout of the logo as big as Simon's face. Simon framed it and hung it above his desk.

The grapevine moved swiftly. "When will *our* logos be ready?" people from diverse companies wanted to know. Simon became the Logo King. Orion offices elsewhere took up logo design. Logos kept existing customers happy and were used to good effect in demonstrations to prospects. Graham Danvers talked excitedly about The Icing Theory of Sales: Provide the icing and the cake will sell itself. The comment I liked best, however, came from Simon Tan: "This is such fun!"

Fun, yes. For me, too. But I'm hiding something in the telling, just as I did in the living. Sleeplessness was not the only indication that something was amiss. My body was letting me down. I kept getting infections in my eyes, then my ears, then my throat. The company GP prescribed repeated courses of antibiotics. But each time an infection would be cleared, a new one would begin; and each time I had less energy to fight it.

Illness had no place in Steven's world. I took the tablets and got on with things. But I started to feel unhinged by things I'd previously taken in my stride, and everyday events became glazed with a sense of unreality. Colours were too vivid, sounds too loud, the Equatorial light too bright.

The last interviews were in Bontang, Kalimantan. I had flown to this remote part of Borneo from Balikpapan on an Irish-built hatchback aircraft, with my briefcase as a seat. Thirty chickens pecked at my feet. In the corner was a sack of mail. The only other passenger was a man in bare feet who said he was the pilot's brother.

The engineers at the LNG plant had assigned me to the guest house. But, when I arrived, it was being redecorated for President Suharto's visit to open the plant, a visit that had been brought forward. Once again, I found myself in huts that housed domestic staff. At first I was disappointed but, when

I stood on the veranda after washing before dinner, I experienced one of those rare and precious moments of splendour in an unexpected place. From where I stood, I had a view of the plant in its entirety, and was close enough to see the details of the storage tanks, the four trains (the exchangers were marked A,B,C,D), a ground flare and, most spectacular of all, a vertical flare – a large white-yellow flame, hissing against the deep blue sky of a tropical dusk.

The plant was a living presence to me. It was there, winking with sunlight, first thing in the morning, and there, smouldering in mystery, before I went to bed. During the days, I learned how it was put together and how it worked. The engineers were all Canadian or American – a huge change from the Oriental engineers I'd been used to dealing with, across language and cultural divides. But the men here spoke so fast, I had to scramble to keep up.

On my last night, I went dancing with Jim Lowell, a start-up engineer from Calgary. "Dancing?" I asked. "You can go dancing here?"

"Sure," he said, and took me to the Red Top discotheque about half an hour by jeep from the plant. One of the hostesses, an Indonesian woman, greeted me by name and laughed at my startled response. "You have the hut next to my sister," she said.

Who back home would believe any of this – the chickens on the flight, the view from the veranda, the nightclub in the middle of the jungle? Yet, to people like Jim, this was everyday life.

"The last LNG project was in Nigeria," he said. "Long way away but pretty much the same. Some of the guys who were there are here, too. You think you'll never see those people again but the same faces keep popping up. The next project's in Bolivia."

"What project is that?" I asked.

What he told me became a memo to Orion's general manager for South America. An Orion Constellation system was sold for use on that project eighteen months later.

Back in Singapore, the office in Robinson Road had relocated from the sixth floor to the eighth – without moving. Lee Kuan Yew had decreed that floor numbering would, from a designated Monday, become standardised. The ground floor would be number one, the second floor number two, the third floor number three – no mezzanines or floors called lobby, and no bowing to Chinese practice of omitting floor number thirteen.

"Do you know how much it's going to cost to get all our stationery reprinted?" Steven muttered.

"While we're reprinting," I said, "can I have 'sales executive' on my card?"

"What?"

"Sales executive. My contract is almost up. I want to stay – but not on the periphery. I'd like to go on line."

"Out of the question," he said.

"It was you who encouraged me to go into the business world," I said, matching his tone.

"I didn't mean sales in this part of the world, for heaven's sake. People have responded to you well, in the role you've performed out here, but sales would be a whole new ball game."

His answer didn't perturb me. I had learned how to wait.

Jonathan was due in Singapore at Christmas. ("Again?" I asked. Steven didn't reply.) The office was frantic. The job of managing customer support had got on top of Ian, rather than the other way around. Lucy was conducting training courses and seminars. Graham was everywhere at once, trying to meet the sales forecasts Steven had set.

The two of them argued almost daily – not in the office; at our flat. I'd go upstairs, but their raised voices would drift up.

"You're trapped behind rose-coloured glasses," Graham said on one occasion, the most heated.

"Bollocks," said Steven.

"First," said Graham, "you have to face the fact that we're in a period of no growth. Second, you must start cutting back. We have too many expats. They have flats, cars, trips back home. We can't afford these people. We have to go local."

"Do you know how long it would take to train new people?" Steven demanded. "Do you know how much income we'd lose while doing that? Your thinking is arse-backwards. You're looking at costs instead of revenue. These are million-dollar systems we're selling. Go *sell* them. I've forecast 40 per cent growth out of Singapore. You're responsible for meeting that target."

"I didn't set the bloody target," Graham shouted. "It's too high. You're living in cloud cuckoo land."

"Is that right," said Steven, his voice low. "Is that *right*. Well, then, if you want to keep living in this land, perhaps *you'd* better become a cloud cuckoo, too."

In the office, Graham and Steven tried to present a united front. But Graham wore his suit jacket all the time, not only when going out, and he wore it buttoned. He wore it as armour.

Steven's armour slipped. His days were still occupied as they had been before by the usual general managerial round of meetings with sales executives, customer support staff, accountants, clients and prospects. But his relaxed charm and easy authority had disappeared.

He gave orders instead of trying to persuade. He snapped at suppliers. He complained about the way the Number Three secretary answered the phone. He sent a blazer back to the drycleaner's because the crease on one of the sleeves wasn't straight enough. He told Sandy Chan to get the rental car agency to give him a new car because the one he'd received upon his return from K.L. was unacceptable.

"In what way?" Sandy asked timidly.

"The car," said Steven, cutting the air with his hand, "has rust, engine trouble, stereo speakers that don't work, sticky brakes, and is basically a heap of shit."

Sandy's voice was loud and firm when she made the call. I could hear her from my desk. "The car has rust," she said, "engine trouble, stereo speakers that don't work, sticky brakes, and is basically a heap of . . ." She faltered. "A heap of no good." After a brief silence, she started on what appeared to be a repetition in Chinese.

I'd never seen Steven rattled like this. One night, a week before Jonathan was due to arrive, he rummaged through the boxes that had been stored, unopened, under the stairs since the move from Hong Kong. He came out holding a Lindis-farne record from the early Seventies, which he played over and over again while sitting on the couch, slumped, his eyes closed as though trying to block out the whole world.

When he finally joined me in bed, he said: "I'm not giving you the attention you deserve, I know, but you don't understand the pressure I'm under."

"How can I?" I asked quietly. "You don't tell me."

"I know that, too." He sighed and hung up his suit. "Graham and Derek won't do what I tell them. They don't realise that *I* have to do what I'm told, too. If we don't perform out here, Jonathan will simply shut the whole South-east Asian operation down.

"Graham accuses me of not being prepared to make what he calls the hard decisions. But my hands are tied. He thinks we should prune the tree. What he doesn't seem to comprehend is that we're in danger of being pulled out by the roots. Graham doesn't believe Jonathan would do that. Jonathan wouldn't think twice about chopping us down. He'd use us for firewood."

"What about the support commitment to customers?"

"Jonathan's interested in sales. What happens after that is of concern to him only insofar as it affects new sales."

"Then why is he so interested in my survey?"

Steven looked at me carefully. "You're sharper than I sometimes give you credit for."

"Is that supposed to be a compliment?"

He chewed on his moustache. "I didn't mean to insult you. Of course Jonathan's interested in the survey. You've done a good job."

"You haven't answered my question."

"I know," he said. "Oh Laurie, I'm so *tired*."

It wasn't like other Orion gatherings. We were in the coffee-shop of the Goodwood Park Hotel, where Jonathan, Adam, Derek, Dick, Christopher and Roger were staying because the Marco Polo was full. Everyone was subdued. Anecdotes were embarked upon half-heartedly, if at all. Waiters moved listlessly across the black-and-white tiled floor.

"A chess board," I said, to break the silence. "The floor looks like a chess board."

"Yes," said Derek unenthusiastically.

"I suppose so," said Graham.

"Chess is for people who can't make moves in real life," said Jonathan. He got up without excusing himself and headed for the toilets.

"Speaking of moves," said Dick, "we might as well all move to Singapore and commute to Saudi, the Gulf, Sydney or Hong Kong. Why does Jonathan need us here again? How are we expected to meet our targets in our regions if we're never *there?*"

"Seconded," said Christopher.

"Thirded," said Roger.

"Oh, for heaven's sake," said Adam.

Jonathan returned, as did the silence, which continued through lunch. During coffee, I gave a summary of what I'd been doing – the reason I'd been invited – and answered a barrage of questions, mainly from Jonathan, who then asked me to go powder my nose. Adam gave me a stare which said: If you intend to say something strident, or even witty, don't.

I left the coffeeshop and circumnavigated the lobby. It was too hot to go out.

When I returned, Jonathan said: "I want you to do some work for us in Australia. Not a survey of existing clients, but some business development, some research into potential markets. What do you say?"

I looked at Steven, but he was absorbed in examining the tablecloth. Roger, with whom I'd be working if I said yes, was just as intently readjusting his tie.

"How long would it be for?" I asked.

"To begin with, shall we say three months?"

I glanced at Adam, who nodded.

"Sounds interesting," I said. "I'd like to think about it."

"You do that," said Jonathan.

The atmosphere did not improve. On Jonathan's last night, we had dinner at the Shangri-La. There were no Orion anecdotes at all. Jonathan told a joke about a prostitute and a donkey. Once again, Adam stared at me in caution, so I did not say anything, just sat there with lava for blood. Jonathan told prostitute jokes for an hour. I developed a sudden interest in crockery and scrutinised all the pieces on the table.

That evening, while undressing for bed, Steven stood in socks and shirt, trousers folded over his arm, and stared at the wall. "The bastards," he said.

"Steve – "

"You don't understand."

"You don't *tell* me."

"The bastards," he said again, and I knew there was no point trying to reach him.

Perhaps I should have tried harder; I don't know. All I do know is that, once again, I felt like I had as a child – so far away from the line of sight as to be almost invisible.

The final report on the survey was almost done, but it was taking longer than it should have done because of continued ear and throat infections, more antibiotics, and something new – occasional shooting pains in my stomach. I had to let Jonathan know if I was going to take up his offer in Sydney. I'd hoped Steven would ask me not to, to stay with him instead. But he didn't mention it. He acted as though Jonathan's offer had never been made.

I wrote lists: of sections in the report to write or check; of phone calls to make, letters to send, bills to pay. I can see the funny side, now, of including "have shower" and "clean contact lenses", but all I could see at the time was what those lists said about things I was avoiding.

"Let's go to Bangkok for New Year's Eve," Steven said. "You've always wanted to stay at the Oriental."

"I'd love to," I said, filled with dread. Would this be Steven's way of bringing about The End of the Affair?

I needed someone to talk to, but whom? It hardly would have been appropriate to confide in Lucy, or anyone else at the office. I had tried to contact Susan several times, despite what I'd regarded as her hostile reaction when I'd joined Orion. But she hadn't answered her phone, returned my calls, or replied to my letters. In that way she was like my mother, but I expected nothing other than that from my mother. Susan had been like an older sister. Her silence hurt me more than I was prepared to admit.

And then a letter from Susan arrived. I recognised her handwriting on the envelope on the mat the minute Steven and I walked through the door one night, late, after dinner at the Sheraton.

"I haven't seen you smile like that for yonks," Steven said as we walked up the stairs.

I opened the letter eagerly, impatient for news of Susan, of *The Age*, of things back home.

"Dear Laurie," the letter said, "I am sorry I have not replied to your letters but I have been depressed. It will not go away. I resigned from the paper. I would have been fired anyway. I moved in with mother and father, into my old room. I wish I could explain more to you. I wish I could explain it to myself."

I stood by the bed, unable to move.

"Are you all right?" Steven asked.

I handed him the letter.

"Well," he said, a little too brightly, "at least she's got her parents. She'll sort herself out."

I thought of the Susan I'd known, with her enthusiasm and energy; and I recognised how manic her behaviour had been at times, how fierce. What had she been covering up? I felt ashamed at not having considered this before.

"Perhaps some people fall apart and stay that way," I said.

"We're all falling apart," Steven said, without looking up. "Some people just hide it better."

That comment didn't seem significant at the time, but it has echoed in my head for years.

I remember a foolscap notepad Steven kept in his briefcase. It was divided into columns headed "Do, Write, Phone, Telex". At the time, I thought it showed how well-organised he was. It didn't occur to me that Steven's lists might embody the same panic as mine. When I picture those lists, in Steven's distinctive vertical handwriting, I feel selfish and bewildered and estranged from him, all over again.

On New Year's Day, in our room at the Oriental, the stomach pains became so bad I could no longer hide them.

When the doctor arrived, I was leaning over the bathroom sink.

"Thank you for coming so promptly," Steven said. "My . . . my . . . *wife* has been in pain all morning."

Later, when the medication to settle my stomach had begun to work, I sat with Steven on the hotel terrace overlooking the Chao Phya river. Steven was reading the *Financial Times*, its pink pages rippling in the wind. I was holding a copy of *The Far Eastern Economic Review*.

Did we look like a happy couple? Or was the situation clear to anyone who happened to look?

"I'll go to Australia," I said suddenly, deciding to take up Adam's offer.

"Great," said Steven.

"Great?"

"It means we won't be losing you from Orion."

"And us?"

Steven didn't reply.

When I look back on when we were together, I think of all the times Steven didn't reply. His silences are with me still. They always will be.

chapter six

At Sydney airport, I cleared immigration and collected my luggage. The eight suitcases I'd taken to Singapore had been whittled to two. I'd given most of my clothes and books away.

It was 7.30 a.m., a Sunday. I didn't feel like going to the hotel. I went to the restaurant for coffee, and stayed there an hour and a half. Why didn't I want to leave the airport? Why didn't I know?

For the first time in months, I wasn't expected to be anywhere. I wasn't due at the office until the next day. I didn't have any work to prepare. There wasn't anyone I had to see.

I wanted to see Susan. There was a flight to Melbourne at ten.

I gave the taxi driver the address on the back of Susan's letter. The street was near Camberwell Junction, where I'd had summer jobs during high school, in grocery stores and cafes.

Burke Road had changed. None of the places I'd worked in were still there. Multi-storey shopping complexes had replaced the old strips of single-storey shops, and the street had the shiny, polished look of older suburbs become fashionable again.

I'd never met Susan's parents. I wasn't even sure they'd know who I was.

Mrs Roth opened the door and stared at the suitcases.

"Hi," I said. "I'm Laurie Michaels."

"But you're in Singapore."

We stood there, each as awkward as the other, until Dr Roth came to the door as well.

"Please come in and please excuse us," he said, his Polish accent muted but still quite strong. "You will see that we are preoccupied."

"I wanted to see Susan. I came straight from the airport."

Dr Roth carried the suitcases into the lounge. "I'm sure Laurie would like a cup of tea, Zosia," he said.

Mrs Roth nodded and disappeared.

"Have you heard from Susan?" he asked.

"Only one letter," I said. "Is she here?"

Dr Roth looked at the palms of his hands. "No," he said, looking up again. "She's at a small psychiatric clinic in St Kilda. It was at her own request. She claims we were trying to punish her."

"How? For what?"

He paused. "I know you're a good friend of Susan's. You have to understand that we're not dealing with the normal Susan here. Logic takes on a different dimension. What she says seems sensible to her, within her own framework. But those of us on the outside – "

"Can I see her?"

"The doctors won't even let us see her. She's heavily sedated."

"What happened?"

Mrs Roth returned with a tray of tea and honey cake. She saw my expression and started to cry.

Dr Roth took the tray and put it on the coffee table. "It's a very easy thing to find labels and explanations," he said. "I do it every day, with my own patients. But when it's your daughter – "

"Susan's angry at herself," said Mrs Roth. "She says she's a failure. Her name in the paper every day on very nice articles – she should be proud. Maybe, I say to myself, it's because she doesn't have a husband, doesn't have children. But she said she didn't want that life. All right, I say, and if she wants that now, it's not too late. In Ziegenhain, after the war, people were older than Susan is now, people who started again – "

"Ziegenhain's not relevant here, Zosia," Dr Roth said, patting her arm.

We were silent. Ziegenhain had been a ghostly presence since my childhood. At the Jewish secondary school I'd attended, many of my friends had had parents who'd passed through Ziegenhain, one of the transit camps set up in Europe for displaced persons after the war. Visas had been arranged there – for England, the United States, South America and, furthest away of all, Australia.

Ziegenhain probably *was* relevant, but in ways that couldn't easily be explained. Dr Roth seemed to be thinking along the same lines, but perhaps he had decided long before that some things are better left to fade.

"Susan's very idealistic," I said.

"So were we," said Dr Roth. "That's why we came to Australia – as far away from the Old World as possible. Australia seemed wonderful to us – the opportunities, the freedom from hatred. You could have anything you wanted here if you worked for it. We encouraged Susan in everything. She had a brilliant future. But maybe reality didn't measure up. Idealism is a good thing, but you have to live in the real world."

Mrs Roth shakily poured some tea. "Susan says about you that you know how to do this, that you know how to live in the world. She wishes she could be like you."

"Be like *me*?" I asked. Susan had been *my* role model.

I couldn't bear to stay much longer. I gave Dr and Mrs Roth the phone number of my office in Sydney, and left feeling covered in shame. My involvement with Steven and Orion had eclipsed everything. I should have been more persistent in trying to contact Susan. I should have been a better friend.

But there wasn't much I could do about that now. I took a taxi to the Hilton, checked in, and collapsed into sleep.

In the evening, I took a taxi to Kew, to the house of my early and middle teens. The house had been sold some months before, when my parents had taken up teaching positions at the University of Toronto. My sister had gone to work as an intern at a hospital in Jerusalem. My brother was on contract as an agricultural adviser somewhere in Africa. Even Rick, from whom I'd soon be divorced, had moved, to Brisbane.

I returned to the Hilton and walked into the bar. A man bought me a drink.

"Where you from?" he asked.

I laughed. He thought I was laughing at him, and moved away. But how could I say I was from Melbourne? How could I explain that I'd become a stranger in my own home town?

The view from Nicolas Wherrett's desk in Orion's office on the nineteenth floor was of the Sydney Opera House wedged between the Gold Fields office tower and the Regent Hotel. Cars sped along the Cahill Expressway in the foreground and, to the far left, was the "clothes hanger" of the Harbour bridge. That view would be blocked, now, by Grosvenor Place, which by then was already half-built.

Among the hardware manuals and computer magazines on Nicolas's desk, propped up against the in-tray, was a framed photograph of a skiing weekend in New Zealand. Nicolas – whom I'd met once, at a hardware conference in Jakarta – was wearing a hat with the Orion logo, and a ski jacket saying

Plug Me In. Steven was in the photograph, too, wearing the same hat and his one-of-the-boys grin.

Nicolas was installing a system in Auckland, where he would be until the beginning of March, and Roger had assigned me the desk. Day one in a new office.

At nine thirty, as arranged, Roger put his head around the door. I got up and walked with him to the corner office, which looked more like a dining room than a place of work. Instead of a desk, he had a heavy oval timber table. Files were kept in binders housed in timber cabinets that looked as though they were designed to hold expensive crockery rather than contracts and telexes. On the wall were framed pages from a fashion magazine, of Felicity modelling strapless evening gowns somewhere in the Caribbean.

"St Kitts," said Roger.

"I'm not sure where that is."

"West Indies. Felicity's not sure where it is, either, and she's *been* there." He picked up his black leather time organiser. "I've written a list of things I want to cover," he said stiffly.

We talked for three hours. "The automobile and pharmaceutical industries are the best places to start, perhaps," Roger said. "The traditional markets – construction, oil – are pretty much under control. Everything's pretty much under control, really."

"It obviously wasn't your idea that I come and work for you," I said.

"As a matter of fact, it wasn't," he said. "You're going to stretch my budget. I'm a salesman. I believe expenditure should go into creating sales. I get my leads by opening my eyes and ears. I don't much go in for market research."

"Or jobs for the girlfriends."

"You said that, not me."

"Being Steven's girlfriend has made things harder for me in

Orion, not easier. But *I'm* trying to build a CV too, you know."

"You're honest," he said. "That's something. Would you like to have lunch?"

At a steakhouse nearby, Roger drank half a bottle of wine before he said: "I've always been afraid of you. All the women I meet through work are secretaries or bookkeepers, with the occasional techo in shirt and jeans indistinguishable from the male techos. Most of the other women I know are models or corporate wives." He poured himself another glass of wine. "Well, I've said all that now. You're here. We should make the most of it."

I was surprised and unsettled when the switchboard operator at *The Age* recognised my voice and asked if I was coming back.

"Who knows!" I said. "Could I speak to Tim Wood?"

"Laurie Michaels," said Tim. "Well, well."

"How are you?"

"Fine. *Where* are you?"

"Sydney. I was wondering if you'd be able to help me with some auto industry research. Just some names and numbers of key executives. You must know them by heart by now. It would save me a lot of time. I'd really appreciate it."

Tim laughed. "I don't know if I should be giving you names and numbers. Susan Roth said you had changed camps, gone over to the enemy."

"Have you seen Susan lately?" I asked, trying to sound casual. How much did people at the paper know?

"She's away travelling, I believe. Not sure where. Tell me – as a public relations person, do you get to fly around in a company jet?"

"I'm not in public relations," I said. "I'm doing business research."

"Just kidding. Jealous, maybe. *Do* you fly around in a company jet?"

"*You* can talk. How many times did you go to Tokyo last year? Or Detroit?"

"Fair enough."

"Can I have those names? I'm not above promising to buy you lunch next time you're in Sydney."

"My choice of restaurant?"

"Sure."

"Eliza's."

"That would cost a whole week's salary!"

"You earn that *much*?"

He gave me the names.

We said goodbye, and I realised how much I missed the good-natured banter of people like Tim. The atmosphere in Orion was different. It wasn't that Orion people took themselves more seriously – most journalists I knew were as intent on climbing ladders as anyone in Orion – but that journalists, by nature or through the practice of their craft, seemed more able to view themselves from the outside.

I remembered something Steve had said once. "You say you envy the way I fit so naturally into my job," he'd said. "It's true – I do feel I'm in the right job. But the fit can be *too* close, sometimes. I wonder how much of me is what I do. I wonder: If I didn't have this job, who would I be?"

"What motivates you?" I'd asked.

"Being successful."

"What is being successful?"

"Winning."

"At what?"

"At whatever game you're playing."

"What's the point, if it's only a game?"

"*Only* a game?" Steven had echoed. "Only a *game?*"

For four weeks, I immersed myself in the car industry. In my report to Roger, I said that Orion Constellation would be appropriate, economically justifiable, and relatively easy to assimilate into existing styles of car industry management, but would involve decision-making from head office which, in almost all cases, meant Tokyo or Detroit.

There was, however, a certain amount of local autonomy, and manufacturing plants of the same company in different parts of the world competed with one another in terms of orders and profits. It made sense, therefore, to push for an Orion sale at the Australian level, and let the managers of Australian operations (who were Japanese or American) persuade head office.

As an appendix, I mentioned the people I'd spoken to, how they fitted into the invisible hierarchy as well as the official one, and whether or not they'd been receptive to descriptions of Orion Constellation.

"You did all this in a *month?*" Roger asked. "How did you make all these contacts?"

He treated me with great solicitude after that and didn't query the three lunches at Eliza's.

A week's research into pharmaceuticals showed that the industry in Australia held little promise so far as Orion was concerned. Most drug manufacturing in the country was under licence, using processes determined in West Germany, Switzerland, or the United States. There was no original research and development being done, partly due to recent increases in taxation and to Government regulation of the industry.

*

"You know how Adam's always on about never handling a piece of paper twice?" Roger asked.

I laughed. Adam was a walking advertisement for every new buzz motto from the books on management which were enjoying an unprecedented boom.

Roger took a perspex tray from the cabinet in his office and put it in front of me. "I must have looked at each of these papers a dozen times or more," he said.

"Ah," I said, "what Steven calls the Too Hard Basket."

"It's not that the things are too hard, really, so much as too fiddly, too time-consuming, and . . ."

"And won't result in a sale tomorrow."

"And won't result in a sale tomorrow, yes."

"Let me have a look at it," I said.

Among the papers in the Too Hard Basket was a letter inviting Orion to contribute to a manual on maintenance engineering of power plants.

"The deadline for this copy has already passed," I said.

"I know," Roger said. "I've tried to write the chapter several times, but I've never been able to get beyond the first few sentences."

"Talk to me about it," I said. "Pretend you're giving a presentation."

"That's easy," he said.

I took notes. Later, I talked to Ian Phillips and some of the other support consultants who worked out of Singapore. (I regretted not feeling comfortable enough to contact Hugh Spurling, who was the most knowledgeable of all.)

It took three days to knock the article into shape and deliver it, as promised, only a week late.

We received an advance copy of the book a couple of weeks later. Orion had a whole chapter, "by Roger Benham". Roger made 100 photocopies and sent them to Orion offices around the world, with a memo acknowledging my "valuable editing".

In the days that followed, I could do no wrong.

But then, at three o'clock on a Wednesday afternoon late in February, Roger stormed into my office with unconcealed rage.

"You little minx," he said, "you could have warned me."

"About what?"

" 'About what,' she says."

"About *what?*"

"Your Machiavellian friend has got himself up as managing director for Asia and Australia now, and a seat on the executive committee in Houston. You bloody could have warned me."

"I don't know anything about it!"

"I don't believe you."

"It's true. We talk on the phone, of course, but he's never even hinted at anything like that."

Roger stared at me. He was ten years older than Steven, and had joined the company even before Steven had. In fact, I'd recently discovered, Roger had been Steven's first boss. Now, Roger would be reporting to Steven.

"Maybe you really don't know," he said. "I suppose I should have realised what was going on at Christmas, in Singapore. Steven Reid is even more of a bastard than I thought." He paused. "I'll be damned if I'm going to let Jonathan and Adam do a Hugh Spurling on me. I'm a part of Orion and I'll stay a part of Orion until the time comes." He walked out.

I rang Singapore. Sandy Chan told me Steven was in Houston. I rang the Sheraton Town and Country Hotel. The telephone rang and rang. It was nearly midnight.

Steven finally answered, an hour and a half later. "Fantastic, isn't it!" he said. "I won't even be reporting to Adam any more. I'll be reporting directly to Jonathan – that is, from June. Adam's going to Holland in June, to get Europe organised. He'll be keeping the Middle East, but he's handing over the rest to me. We've been out celebrating."

"I wish I'd been there to celebrate with you!" I said, trying to sound chirpy and light.

"You wouldn't have liked it. Jonathan took us to a strip joint. All these blondes here! Every time you turn around, you fall in love."

Was Steven aware of the cruelty of this remark? "Roger's very upset," I said.

"He'll get over it."

"I'm not so sure."

And, indeed, Roger didn't get over it. At the end of the week, he announced his return to London, to take over as UK sales manager from a man who had already been moved sideways.

Not long afterwards, Graham told me on the phone that Jonathan had originally promised Roger the MD's job for Asia/ Australia and a place on the executive committee. "Adam and Steven flew to Houston immediately," Graham said. "I don't know what they said to Jonathan to change his mind, but I can guess. They would have said something about some people having outmoded ethical standards that might get in the way."

"Get in the way of what?"

Graham took a while to reply. "I'm not totally clear on that myself," he said.

Roger and Felicity made preparations to leave – Roger, with a heaviness of step that hadn't been there before; Felicity, with an eagerness that bordered on the rude. She gave a farewell dinner for the office, where she served biscuits with lettuce and cheese while we waited for a meal that never came. The furniture had already been packed, and we stood around unsure what to do with ourselves.

Everyone was unsettled at work, too, but quickly adjusted to the prospect of new loyalties. Rumours were thick as to who might take over from Roger, but no one knew. Steven set about finding a replacement. He said he'd fill the gap between Roger's departure and the new appointment himself.

"It's crazy," he told me on the phone. "I've finally moved into a new flat I really like, and now I won't be able to spend time in it."

"You didn't tell me about a new flat."

"Didn't I? It's in Leonie Hill Road. Much better than the old one I had."

"The old flat you had? The old flat *you* had?"

"It's a real bachelor pad."

"Do you say these things deliberately?" I screamed.

Steven's fake jovial tone disappeared. "We're stringing this out," he said. "It's over. You're just not the right person. I wish you were."

I didn't respond.

"Say something," he said. "What are you thinking?"

What I was thinking was: Graham would be proud of you. You've made a decision.

"I'm not thinking anything at all," I said. "Goodbye."

It was seven o'clock. Everyone else in the office had gone home. I organised my papers, which didn't take long because it wasn't clear what I was supposed to be working on. Roger had suggested I investigate the potential for Orion Constellation in aircraft maintenance, but he'd been vague about it at the time, and he certainly wasn't interested in talking about it now.

What was I doing here? I'd been living in Steven's world, on his terms. I'd just been banished, yet I was still working for Orion. What was I *doing* here? I went into Roger's room and watched night fall across the harbour and the lights come on.

At night, in my dreams, I had no face. Without the lipstick, blusher and mascara of my waking hours, my face faded into the invisibility I had begun to dread.

I had to go somewhere else, but where? I'd gone to Hong Kong and ended up here, back in Australia. Somewhere along the way I'd lost a man I loved, my profession, and a sense of who I was. I'd also lost a best friend. Each week, I had rung the Roths, only to be told that Susan was still not allowed visitors.

Perhaps not surprisingly, given my upbringing, I thought of returning to the comforting structures of university as a way of starting again. Susan and I had talked, often, about doing the master's in journalism at Columbia University in New York as a way of getting a newspaper job in the States, but we'd never applied. Perhaps we were afraid we wouldn't get in – or, worse, that only one of us would.

I picked up the phone, asked international directory for the Columbia University graduate school of journalism and, as it was 1 a.m. – well within office hours, New York time – made the call. The closing date for applications had just passed, I was told, but the school would consider a late application if it arrived within the next few days.

In the morning, I rang Tim Woods and asked him to photocopy some articles from my personal cuttings file in the newspaper library. He faxed them before lunch. I put them into a package with a CV I'd prepared, the names of three referees I'd contacted that morning, and a required piece on "Why journalism matters" that I'd written during the night. The courier picked up the parcel at half past two.

Afterwards, I walked through Martin Place and watched pigeons scudding against the imposing stone facades of banks. A woman in shorts and a halter-neck top ambled by, humming. She seemed so *at ease* with herself, not the sort of person who would misplace her face.

I thought of Susan and stopped at a phone booth. There seemed little point in ringing her parents again. Instead, I asked for Melbourne directory, then rang the St Kilda clinic direct. The receptionist put me on to a nurse, who transferred me to another, who passed me to a third. That nurse kept me waiting a few minutes while she conferred with someone else. "Yes," she said finally, "it might be good for Susan to see you. She has mentioned your name."

I booked a seat on the four o'clock plane.

In the well-tended grounds of what had once been a grand colonial home, Susan said: "Do you notice how slow I am." There was no inflection at the end of the question, so it sounded like a statement. Her speech was monotonous and flat.

"Perhaps that's part of the recovery process," I said uncertainly.

Susan leaned forward. "It's all the drugs. There are so many of them, I can't remember their names. I can't remember much of anything. Everyone here is trying very hard to help me, but when I wake up in the morning, I look out the window at the garden and it doesn't look real. The trees sort of *shimmer*." She glanced at a nurse who was strolling with another patient nearby. "Sometimes the trees talk to me, but you mustn't tell the nurses that. They nod and tell the doctors, who give me more drugs."

Susan closed her eyes, and we spent much of the afternoon just sitting there, sweating in the heat. When visiting time had ended, I walked her inside, to a room where people sat without talking, some of them watching television, but most of them staring at visions of their own.

The nurse from the garden accompanied me to the front door. "Susan responded well," she said. "It would be good for her to see you again."

"Could I take her to a film tomorrow night?"

The nurse hesitated. "If you promise not to leave her alone, not even for a minute."

"Yes," I said. "Thank you."

I watched as she walked inside. "Well," I would have said to Susan, "here I am – about to become my sister's keeper!" But the Susan I could have told this to seemed to have got lost for a while. I started walking to the tram – a tram Susan and I had taken once, for coffee on The Esplanade, after a rally we'd covered at the St Kilda town hall. The Susan of that day – laughing, telling jokes – was so vivid a presence that I stopped, transfixed, unable to move. Then I cried and felt the stiffness in my spine and neck subside. But what good did that do Susan?

Susan slept through most of the film she'd chosen, Franco Zeffirelli's *La Traviata*. Afterwards, trying to provide enough talk and cheerfulness for two, I took her to Pancake House, where we'd often gorged ourselves on buckwheat and blueberries.

In the cool air of the courtyard, a respite from the day's

relentless heat, I chattered about the times we'd been here before. Susan's concentration came and went, but I kept up the monologue.

"I'm thinking of going to Columbia," I said. "Why don't you come with me?"

She didn't respond.

"Or come for a visit."

Still no response.

"That is, if I get accepted. You could probably line up some pieces for *The Age* or one of the glossies."

The pancakes arrived. Susan took one bite and pushed hers away. "I don't believe in a future like that," she said. "I'm not able to concentrate long enough to read the 'Odd Spot' in *The Age*."

"But this is only temporary."

Susan leaned forward, in the same urgent, secretive gesture of the day before. "You know what the worst thing is?"

"What?"

She leaned back again. "When you want to scream and you can't."

We ate our pancakes in silence. Susan didn't finish hers. When I dropped her off in a taxi, I gave her the phone numbers of the office and the serviced apartment in Sydney. "Ring reverse charges any time you want. Will you do that?"

She shrugged.

"I care about you, Susan."

"Why?"

"Because you're my friend."

She started to cry, doing nothing to check the tears or wipe them away; she simply let them fall. "But I'm not the same person any more."

"You will be."

"How?"

The nurse came towards us and took Susan's arm.

chapter seven

As I walked through the lobby of The Regent in Sydney, I thought of all the Thai, Korean, Filipina, Indonesian and Chinese women my own age whom I'd seen doing what I was doing now – heading straight for the lifts without picking up a key, to enter a room booked in someone else's name. (I'd seen some of these women at breakfast next morning, alone, eating pieces of toast with chopsticks, or pancakes with their hands.)

Steven opened the door. We faced each other awkwardly. "I hoped you'd be at the airport," he said. "Here, give us a hug."

We went down to the coffeeshop. The man who showed us to the table and the waiter who took our order were both Hong Kong Chinese. Steven looked around at the beige walls and the peach-coloured tablecloths. "I must have made a mistake," he said. "This is clearly The Regent in Kowloon."

"When I was in Vancouver," I said (laughing at myself for the predictable *when I was in*), "doing a story for *ABT*, all the people on the desk at the Holiday Inn were Hong Kong Chinese. On my registration card, for place of residence, I wrote Hong Kong. The check-in staff collapsed in mirth. I could see their point."

Steven was smiling. "Do you miss journalism?"

"Sometimes."

"I like it when you talk about it."

"You *hate* journalism."

"Not totally true. It's what first attracted me to you, after all."

"You won't win me so easily, you know."

"It's worth a try."

"Why?"

"Sometimes I make a mental note to tell you things when I get home, but when I get home you're not there."

I smiled at him but did not trust myself to speak.

"Roger hasn't stopped talking about how useful you've been," he said. "Anyone would have thought it was *his* idea you come out here."

"As far as Roger's concerned, you're the biggest bastard who ever walked."

Steven stopped smiling. "He has to grow up."

"That's quite something," I said, "coming from you."

Leaning across the table, he kissed me on the mouth.

"You've taken me by surprise," I said.

"I'm taking you upstairs," he said.

We were twenty minutes late for dinner with Roger and Felicity at Doyle's in Watson's Bay. I was amazed that Steven had organised the dinner. "Appearances have to be maintained," he said.

Roger looked at me, at Steven, then at me again, and said: "I thought you two had split up."

Steven pretended not to hear. He turned to Felicity and said: "How I envy you, going back to the UK! Oh, for a steak and kidney pie!"

"I would have thought black pudding was more to your taste," Roger said.

"Black pudding's just an accompaniment," Steven said, "even in Newcastle. It's how good the meat is that counts."

Felicity took an emery board from her handbag and started filing her nails.

Roger and Steve talked about soccer and ate quickly, eager to get the meal behind them so they'd be able to mention it if anyone asked. Felicity and I talked about shoes.

The Benhams drove us home, Steven to The Regent, me to the apartment in Oxford Street.

The phone was ringing when I walked in. "This is stupid," Steven said. "Why don't you jump in a taxi?"

"Taxis at midnight," I said, thinking of the different harbour view on the way to Jardine's Lookout. "Why don't you come here?"

"I'm on the 6.55 a.m. to Melbourne."

"On a Sunday?"

"I have to talk to some people about the new Orion software modules."

"Software modules?"

"They haven't been announced yet. Pre-packaged applications. They're going to be dynamite in Asia, but I'm not so sure about Australia. I want to get a few opinions, off the record. Is that the right term?"

"Yes. Was this afternoon off the record, too?"

"Not for me, it wasn't."

"Taxis at midnight," I said again.

The telephone reminder call came at 4.45 a.m., five minutes after Steven's alarm had gone off. Breakfast came at 5.05. Steve left the room at 5.45 to go to the airport. It was just like old times. I stayed in bed, drifting in and out of sleep.

When I woke, it was almost nine. On the pillow was a note: "Will you help me fight the pirates?"

In the office Monday morning, Steven read the report I'd

prepared on Australian opportunities for Orion in aircraft maintenance. "This looks reasonable," he said.

At dinner, he said: "I like your hair like that."

"I always wear my hair like this."

"I like it."

In bed, he was ardent and affectionate.

"What has gone *right*?" I asked.

He laughed. "I must remember that. Next time Graham makes a sale – he hasn't made one for quite a while – I'll keep a perfectly straight face and say: What has gone *right*?"

"How *is* Graham?"

"Graham's Graham. Nothing's changed with him."

"What has changed with *you*?"

Steven shifted from his back to his side and faced me square-on. "I *am* trying to change, you know. I'm nearly thirty-two. I can't be Peter Pan for ever. You keep telling me that, and you're right. It's time to make some sort of emotional commitment."

"Emotional commitments don't get made by executive decision."

Steven looked at me in a way I hadn't seen before. "Decisions aren't what's at issue here," he said. "Emotions are. Finding them."

"*Finding* them?"

"Do you think that's so unusual? I suspect quite a lot of people are this way. That's what I admire about you – you care about things."

"What are you talking about? *You* care about things. You sure as hell care about what happens in the company."

"That's different. That's business. Business is a game. Emotions are serious. That's why they're so frightening. Two years in Saudi Arabia didn't help much, either."

He got out of bed and walked to the window. "I'm glad I

left that bloody place," he said. He clenched and unclenched his fists then turned around, his body silhouetted against an indigo sky. "I, uh, want to make a commitment to you."

"Do you mean this, or do you feel you *ought* to mean it?"

Steven's face crumpled; for a moment it seemed he might cry. "For God's sake," he said, "let me *try*."

I looked at this man, standing at the window, without a suit, a shirt or a briefcase, his hair everywhichway instead of blow-dried into place.

"We live in separate countries," I said.

"That's geography."

I closed my eyes and nodded.

"So we're back together? That's settled, then. Yippee! Let's order room service."

Steven stayed ten days, at the end of which Howard G. Crann arrived from "Hooston, Tayxus", wearing cowboy boots, a business suit, and a Stetson. I had my doubts about how successful Howard would be – a Stetson in the land of the Akubra – but there was little point telling Steven that now. Howard had not, in fact, been Steven's first choice. Three other Orion executives had turned down the job, saying Australia was too far away.

"No balls," was all Steven had said about them, but I knew from his tone of voice that those people would never be given a chance in Asia or Australia again, if Steven had a say. He took their rejection of the job almost as a rejection of him. Perhaps, partly, it was.

Steven returned to Singapore, to let Howard "run the ranch". I stayed in Sydney to "help Howard". My contract would expire early in April. We hadn't talked about what would happen afterwards. It really *was* like old times.

*

"We've decided not to release the software modules in Oz," Steven said on the phone from Singapore, "but we're going to launch them here in a couple of weeks, at a users' meeting. It's a new group, just formed. It's called Asian Engineers In Orion Using."

"That's a strange name," I said.

"The Koreans came up with it. Write down the initials."

I did. "A.E.I.O.U.," I said.

"Don't you think that's a riot? Planning engineers hold projects together like vowels hold words together. The first time I heard that, I was so stunned I forgot to laugh. Now I laugh."

"I think it's endearing," I said.

"It will make the group look foolish. It will make *us* look foolish."

"Do you think so? It's a good line. It's a good promotion opportunity. New regional organisation, first meeting. Singapore *loves* seeing itself as a regional centre. I could get you page three of the *Business Times* and page one of the business section of the *Straits Times*, not to mention trade magazines, possibly even TV, if you got the relevant minister to open the meeting."

"Ogden Burroughs would go off his head."

"All it would cost would be a month's fees and an airfare. No accommodation expenses. Cheap."

"That's not the point. It's the jobs-for-the-girlfriends thing."

"Not *still*, surely! Even Jonathan has commented about my work."

"Ogden's a bean counter. Bean counters are interested in beans. You're not actually growing beans. You're . . . I guess you're providing fertiliser."

"That can be taken two ways."

"I didn't mean it like that."

"You'd be passing up a good opportunity."

Steven was quiet a moment. "There are other factors involved which might swing it," he said. "It does have potential."

"Potential is meaningless unless you realise it."

Steven laughed. "You've been reading a manual on how to sell."

"I don't need to. I'm talking to one."

"I want to discuss it with Adam first."

"Ah, now I know you're taking me seriously. Oh Adam, who art in an aeroplane somewhere . . ."

"Very funny. I'll talk to you later."

Only after Steven had put down the phone did I wonder what those "other factors" might be.

Adam rang that evening. "Give me your pitch," he said.

I did.

"When will you know if you've got into Princeton?"

"Columbia. Late April."

"Can you do the publicity launch in a month?"

"Yes."

"You've got it."

"Great!"

"Do you know why the engineers' group calls itself A.E.I.O.U.?"

"Yes. I think it's cute."

"I'm not looking forward to explaining it to the executive committee. They already think Asia's a bit of a joke as it is. Annual sales in the whole of Asia, Australia and New Zealand currently count for less than half the number of sales in Texas."

"Yes, but in Texas they speak English as their first language."

"Don't you believe it," said Adam. "Last time I flew into

Houston, the customs chap looked at my passport and said: 'What brings an English gentleman to this former colony?' I said: 'I've come to take it back.' Then he mumbled something to a colleague nearby which I didn't understand *at all*."

Changi! Its splendid gleaming transience! No responsibilities or anxieties – only the streamlined realities of passport control and luggage belts, the hard-edged clarity of detachment.

Steve's new apartment was on the twelfth floor. The view was of other residential towers, their blazing windows forming geometric patterns of light against a deep blue sky. The effect was the same as the airport – shiny, hi-tech, detached, self-contained.

A birthday card taped to the door said: "Will ring you from Houston, there's yoghurt in the fridge."

The flat was cosy rather than large, with white walls, polished timber floors, and steps leading to a dining area overlooking the lounge. There were batik prints from Jogjakarta, oversized silk cushions from Bangkok, and some woven rugs from Baguio.

In the bedroom were watercolours of the Lake District and a pile of climbing magazines. In what was supposed to be a second bedroom were the boxes from Hong Kong, still unpacked from their previous move. Leaning in a corner were three pairs of skis.

On a bookshelf in the lounge were well-thumbed business texts, and novels by James Clavell, Frederick Forsyth and John le Carré. Next to the stereo were some Bob Seger records. There was nothing of me in the flat – not a photograph, a letter, a comb or a skirt.

I put my suits in the cupboard, a paperback on the table

next to what was always my side of the bed, cosmetics in the bathroom, and a terry-towelling bathrobe next to Steven's matching one on the back of the bedroom door.

It's not time so much by which we remember things but place. I stood by the window of my old office in Robinson Road and looked down on the roof of the Telok Ayer market. I had a sense of being back home, something I hadn't felt in Sydney or even in Melbourne. This was silly – I was an outsider here. Perhaps that was the point.

Steven was due back at the weekend, and I hoped to have a media strategy prepared by the time he arrived. Lucy had arrangements for the product launch well under control and had also helped the A.E.I.O.U. committee organise its meeting.

"I've been trying desperately to get them to change their name," she said, "but they're quite, quite set on it."

Lucy was thinner than she'd been three months before, and her customary cheeriness seemed a bit forced. "Ian is awfully bogged down," she said, in response to a question I hadn't asked. "He's short-staffed, of course, but he could be more efficient, I think. On the other hand, I do admire his enthusiasm."

I had dinner with Lucy and Ian every night. During the day, I compiled a media list of reporters and editors, and mapped out what we would want to say in press releases and interviews to different publications. There were new client files to read and updates on existing clients. I had hoped to talk to Graham, but he was in Jakarta, where he would remain until early the following week.

The night before Steve was due back from Houston, I rang him at the Sheraton Town and Country, 8 a.m. his time.

"Hello," he said. "I've got to dash. I'll keep buttoning my shirt."

"The meetings with Jonathan – how have they gone?"

"Can't talk. No time."

His voice was low and deep, the way it was when things were not as he'd wish – so different from the relaxed voice in Sydney. A familiar anxiety gripped my throat. I could feel my neck begin to swell. I willed it to go down.

Steven gave the opening speech at the software modules launch wearing a grey-and-blue seersucker suit he must have bought in Houston. He seemed to be unveiling a new persona to go with it.

"Look at these sexy little numbers," he said, pointing to the software kits lined up on a table in front of him, each with a distinctive colour. "This curvy blonde, this smouldering brunette, this bouncy redhead. And now, this one – well, it's blue, what the hell, they're all the same in the dark, right?"

I glanced along the seats in the front row, and could see that Lucy had been irritated by the remark too. But Lucy and I were the only women there, and the banter, of course, had not been designed to appeal to *us*.

Certainly, it was going down well with the engineers of the A.E.I.O.U. Each comment had been greeted with laughter several times – first, by those who had understood it immediately, then by those for whom the comments were translated by colleagues into Korean, Indonesian, and Japanese. The laughter made its way along the rows of seats, a language virus.

During the next few days, Steven told some immensely tacky jokes that I'd heard before, from Jonathan. But they were a small price to pay for cuddles in the morning, songs in the shower, the BBC World Service during the drive to work, and the wait for the lift.

"It gets better the higher up you go," he said one morning.

"The *lift*?"

"The ladder. You're no longer bogged down by stupid, petty details. You're able, finally, to get away from the trees and look at the forest."

"And what does the forest look like?"

Steven laughed. "I suppose," he said, "like a bunch of trees!"

The reception room at the Goodwood Park Hotel was full. Reporters leafed through their press kits. Steven, Graham, and some techos from Houston gave short, sharp speeches then answered questions. I sat next to one of the techos, behind a card with my name and the title, "Public Affairs Manager". Everything was going as planned.

But then a young reporter from the *Singapore Monitor* got up and said: "How much does a project have to be worth before buying Orion Constellation becomes economically justified?"

This was the question that had started it all! This was why I was sitting here now.

Steven and Graham looked at each other.

"Perhaps I can help answer that," I said, glancing at some pages I'd prepared. "Let me outline Orion's clients in the region and the projects in which they're involved." Along the way, I mentioned the values of some of the projects, but only those I'd marked with an asterisk. The asterisks meant the values were common knowledge.

The reporter looked pleased and wrote it all down. Only later would he realise that I hadn't answered the question.

I thought of Tim Wood ("Well," he'd say, "*now* do you get to fly in a company jet?"), and of something the novelist Kurt Vonnegut once said: "We are who we pretend to be, so we must be careful who we pretend to be."

The *Business Times* ran a story on page three, with photographs of Graham and Steve. The *Straits Times* had a piece on the front page of its business section, alongside an interview with the president of A.E.I.O.U. ("Planning engineers hold projects together like vowels hold words together," was the lead.) The *Singapore Monitor* carried a long and somewhat jumbled account on page five.

We'd have to wait and see how we'd fare in the weekly and trade magazines, but the office phones had started to ring already.

"Prospects are calling *us*!" said Steven. "The power of the press!"

"You've changed your tune," I said.

"Look who's talking," he replied, taking from his briefcase the Public Affairs Manager card I'd purposely left behind at the Goodwood Park. "I do believe I'm talking to a woman who said she'd never do PR."

Steven threw a twig into Selat Johor, the stretch of water separating Singapore from Malaysia to the north. The beach was rocky, sparse. We had sat down on the rocks after a dinner of Ponggol's famous chili crab, and Steven had started breaking off twigs, throwing them into the sea.

"I used to do this in the Scouts," he said.

"How long had you been in the Scouts before you started organising the other boys?"

"How did you know that?" he asked.

I laughed.

"Well, it was partly because I was the third person in my area to join," he said. "Getting in early gives you an edge. The same thing happened for me in Orion."

"They're similar organisations."

"Do you think so? I hadn't thought of that before." He aimed another twig. "Did you belong to the Brownies?"

"No. I went, once. Refused to go back."

"That's a pity," he said. "It's important to learn about groups. That's how the world functions."

I was silent. In the groups I'd belonged to over the years, I'd been uneasy about group pressures and rituals, and had felt separate and disliked, excluded and scornful, all at the same time.

"I missed Scouts when I left," Steven said. "Clubs at university weren't the same. In fact, I didn't enjoy university at all, until I started the MBA. That was a terrific couple of years. But then there was the terrible time with the PhD, which came to a head when I caught chicken pox from one of the students I tutored in maths."

It was so rare to hear Steven talk about his life like this. I sat and listened to his soft, lilting voice against the night's swish of the sea.

"Two weeks lying in my damp Birmingham bedsit," he continued, "wondering what to do. Finally, I quit, and spent the summer on the dole. I moved in with a girl called Jennifer. She was on the dole wondering what to do, too. She tried to teach me about feminism. What I learned, however, was that women never want what they say they want. One day, I saw an ad for sales traineeships with Xerox."

He stopped, and I was afraid he didn't want to talk any more. But then it became clear that he was simply momentarily absorbed in memories of an earlier self.

"Working for Xerox was the most daunting thing I've ever done," he said. "I was painfully shy, and there I was, knocking on doors in Lancashire, in constant drizzle, asking: 'Do yer want ter buy a photocopier?' Each afternoon, I'd think: 'It's four thirty again, I want to go home.' But the offices were open another hour yet, so I kept going. Wore out five pairs of shoes.

"At the end of two years, I wasn't shy any more. I knew an awful lot about different types of businesses. Most importantly, I learned that selling is about listening and making suggestions. On weekends, I went rock climbing with Nigel – I'd like you to meet him one day – in the Lake District."

Steven took a breath. "Then I saw another ad, for a company I'd never heard of – Orion. It was for a sales rep to cover the North and North-west. 'Jackpot,' I thought, 'I'll be able to live in the Lake District.'

"I went down to London to see them. 'Them' was Jonathan, Ted, Max James and Roger Benham, in a tiny office near Euston Square. They hired me. But my plan misfired because Jonathan transferred me to London after six months, and by then I was too caught up in Orion not to go. I commuted to the Lakes at weekends, which was stupid. I wasn't really living in one place or t'other – I was living in my car.

"Adam had joined by then. He sent me to Saudi Arabia. It was a mad time but the right time. The Saudi Government was awarding new construction jobs every half-hour. The orders came faster than I could write up the contracts.

"And then the bottom fell out of the oil boom. Work on the projects stopped, and I could see it was time to get out. Adam offered me Hong Kong. I jumped at it."

Steven smiled and threw the last twig into the sea. "You know the rest," he said.

I smiled, too. "Except for what happened at Christmas."

Steven stopped smiling. "It's getting late," he said. "We'd best start heading back."

The champagne and noodles were Steven's idea. They were served in the office after work to celebrate two sales of Orion Constellation systems worth half a million US dollars each.

Steven gave a short speech congratulating the two sales execs who had clinched the sales, which had taken more than a year. Everyone clapped. Steve then eulogised the software support consultants, the hardware engineers, the bookkeepers, the secretaries, the mail boy and, finally, the office Auntie.

By that stage, the clapping had become a little less vigorous, a little more forced. But glasses were refilled; Steve told jokes; and most people laughed happily enough whether they understood the jokes or not. Except for Graham, standing at the far end of the room with his arms crossed. He was watching Steven the way I remembered Hugh Spurling watching me.

The phone was ringing when Steven and I got home.

"Just once," I said. "Just once, I wish we could have the evening to ourselves."

Steven picked up the receiver. "I'll hear you out, Graham," he said, "but I won't promise anything."

There was a long pause, and then: "Of *course* they didn't get the sales themselves. *We* know that. *They* know that. The party was for office morale. I do *not* intend to fire the reps. They *will* provide leads of their own, given time. I hired them; I intend to give them a chance. The same goes for Ian Phillips."

The next day, after everyone had left work except Steven, Graham and me, I heard Graham shouting in Steven's office.

"The support side's in disintegration mode," he said. "Ian's got to go."

"I will tell you again," Steven said. "You haven't given Ian enough time."

"Time is money, money is time."

"Very droll."

"They're both running out. Your procrastination is costing us badly."

There was a silence. I pictured Steven staring at Graham fixedly, and Graham crossing his arms. "Maybe so," Steven said at last, "but I'm the boss."

"For now, yes."

"Are you threatening me?"

The phone rang, and Steven said: "Yes, hello Adam, no, that's fine."

Graham walked out of Steven's office and through the glass doors to the lift, without collecting his jacket.

During working hours, however, Steven and Graham were civil to each other and presented themselves to the rest of the office as a team. I sat at my desk quietly, writing articles for trade magazines on the new Orion clients and compiling more quotable quotes for sales presentations. It was almost the end of April. I was waiting to hear whether or not I'd been accepted at Columbia, and my month's contract with Orion in Singapore was drawing to a close. I wondered what I'd be doing a few weeks hence. Neither Adam nor Steven had mentioned the end of my contract, and Steve had said nothing about wanting me to stay. All there was was Now – wide, significant, full of possibility. Life in the present tense. This was the secret of Peter Pan; this was the charm of Peter Pan; this was the pathology of Peter Pan. I was beginning to understand.

And then Steven's uncle died. The news shook Steven more than I could have imagined. His head dropped on to his chest. "Gone," he said, "dead." And I realised that this was the first death he'd had to face.

He left next evening to attend the funeral in Newcastle. I watched him go through the immigration barrier at Changi, clutching suit-carrier and briefcase, staring at the floor.

Airports. So many of my memories of Steven are at airports.

I found out from Sandy Chan which flight Steven was coming back on. In the week he'd been away, I'd done some work, at Steven's suggestion, for Derek Williams in Hong Kong. I booked a return flight that would get in minutes before Steve's. But I hadn't counted on our aircrafts docking at opposite ends of the terminal. I clutched my suit-carrier and ran.

Steven was just emerging from the aircraft into the connecting bridge, his shoulders drooping. But when he saw me he grinned, straightened up and quickened his pace. When he reached me, he put down his bags and gave me a hug, not noticing we were in people's way.

In the taxi, Steven said: "Do you think I'm selfish?"

"Perhaps a little," I said. "Why?"

"At the funeral, my aunt said I should think of my mother more. I didn't take much notice. But Adam and I had a drunken evening in London, before I caught the plane, and he shouted at me that I never think about anyone else. Do you think that's true?"

"You've sprung this on me. You've caught me unaware."

"Do you think it's *true?*"

"Perhaps."

Steven stared straight ahead. "I'm going to change or pack it in," he said.

"You *know* you won't pack it in. And I doubt you'll change."

Steven turned his face to the side. Outside the windows were new high-rise housing estates that Orion Constellation systems were helping to build.

When the Number Three secretary put the letter from Columbia on my desk, I set it aside and glanced at its New York postmark for almost an hour before opening it. I wasn't sure what I wanted it to say.

"Dear Ms Michaels," I read. "We are delighted . . ."

I took the letter into Steven's office.

"I don't have to go," I said. "It's not that important. Just ask me to stay."

"Can we talk about this later?"

"Of course. Sorry."

The day passed in a fog of apprehension. After dinner, Steve said: "I can't ask you to stay. It's too big a responsibility."

I looked at him, but what I saw was the white-yellow flame of the vertical flare in Bontang. "So what am I supposed to *do?*"

"It's up to you."

"Graham's right. You're incapable of making decisions."

"Graham's got nothing to do with this."

I grabbed him by the shoulders and forced him to look at me. "Steven, do you love me?"

"I don't know. I think so, yes."

"Do you want me to *stay?*"

Steven dropped his head on to his chest, in a gesture that was becoming a habit.

I took my hands away. My head was expanding, the walls were closing in. "I think I'll get ready for bed," I said.

"So you got into Princeton," said Adam.

"Columbia," I said into the phone.

"I'd like you to work for me in Holland."

I laughed. "There's always the Adam factor, isn't there!"

"What do you mean? Never mind. We need to set up marketing services almost from scratch. Not just here – the whole of Europe."

"I'll be starting at Columbia in four months."

"Maybe we'll talk you out of that."

"The whole of Europe?"

"I left out Scandinavia."

"Sounds a little vague."

"All my ideas sound vague initially."

"I know."

"And then they're in vogue," he said. "In *vogue!*" Adam laughed at his joke, his irresistible hearty laugh.

"What the hell," I said.

"I knew you'd say yes. You start next week. I've arranged for you to spend a few days in Abu Dhabi on your way, to write a report on a fabrication yard there. Christopher Kendall has been on at me about it for weeks."

At the end of the call, I walked to the window and looked down at Telok Ayer Market. Office workers – Chinese, Malay, Indian and a few Europeans – walked in and out, some slowly, some briskly, to buy lunch from the hawker stalls for which Singapore was famous. Steven was in his office. I had no idea what was on his mind.

At 6 p.m., Steven emerged from the bathroom, drying himself

as he walked. We'd made love briskly, so that he wouldn't be late for the seven thirty to Jakarta.

"I was sad this afternoon when you told me you'd taken Adam's offer," he said.

"Come *on*!"

"I know what I said a few days ago," he continued, while stepping into trousers. "But that was talking about four months' time, not next week."

"And when the four months had *become* next week?"

Steven shrugged. "Perhaps I hoped you'd stay."

"Hoped I'd stay?" I echoed, feeling helpless.

"Well, anyway," he said, tucking a shirt into his trousers and buckling his belt, "I'll see you in Amsterdam June or July." He packed a clean shirt into his suit-carrier and did up the zip. "The next executive committee meeting is going to be there."

I watched while Steven fetched his bag of toiletries from the bathroom and put it in the suit-carrier pocket designed for it. "Whose idea was it to hold the meeting there?" I asked, although I knew what the answer would be.

"Adam's."

There are people in all our lives who make a crucial difference to where, or who, we find ourselves. Adam, clearly, was going to be such a person for me.

Abu Dhabi was flat and sandy, with occasional public plots of tropical greenery that looked out of place.

"You see Indian gardeners out with their watering cans twice a day," Liz Kendall said, turning to face me in the back seat.

The car sped past white- and cream-coloured concrete

apartment blocks, ground floors given over to shops with aluminium roll-up fronts.

Eleven hours before, I'd left the flat in Singapore and had gone to the airport alone. Steve had not yet returned from Jakarta; we'd said our farewells on the phone. Lucy, who'd grown fatter and seemed restless, was in Tokyo. Ian, the thinnest I could remember, was "putting out fires" somewhere in Kalimantan.

"This is the *corniche*," said Christopher. Men in traditional white Arab robes walked hand-in-hand along a path which overlooked the sea. Where were the women? I had the eerie sense of women watching from windows, through veils.

The next day was Sunday, a working day in the Gulf. I sat in the back of a motorboat that Christopher had arranged to take me to Sadiyat island, to the fabrication yard of the National Petroleum Construction Company. I watched the towers of Abu Dhabi shrink behind me in a blaze of sun. Not long afterwards, the structures of the fabrication yard came into view.

The yard was owned jointly by the Abu Dhabi National Oil Company and a Lebanese company now based in Athens. Orion Constellation had been used in the yard for more than three years. Steven had made the sale.

The system was being used well, by engineers – mostly Palestinian – who knew what they were doing and spoke English well. By early afternoon, the day had become a social event. A large group of us adjourned for lunch at The Club, formerly The British Club and still looking very much the part, with a timber-panelled air-conditioned bar and a restaurant full of starched tablecloths.

"Do you know many Orion people in the Gulf?" asked

one of the senior planning engineers, an American-trained Palestinian from Beirut.

"A few," I said. "Christopher Kendall, of course, and Dick Staunton in Riyadh."

"You've been to *Saudi Arabia?*"

"No," I said. "I hoped to be able to go there, but I was denied a visa. I've seen Dick in Singapore and Hong Kong. I also know a couple of people who used to work in Saudi Arabia – Steven Reid, for example."

"Ah yes," he said. "Steven Reid. Very sharp. I hear he's in Singapore now. Does he wear his tie and jacket there? He's the only Englishman I've ever met who wore a jacket in the Gulf. Never mind how hot it got, it was always Steven Reid in a jacket."

The image of Steven in the Gulf – jacket, tie, despite the heat – was so real that something in me was laid to rest. The Gulf had been Steven's life before me. Now I had been here, too, and that was enough.

part two:
europe

chapter eight

Schiphol isn't grand like Changi – no interior waterfalls, atriums or marbled surfaces. But its low ceilings and moving walkways are efficient, anonymous, exhilarating.

It was 7 a.m., 22nd of May. My suit-carrier hung heavily from one shoulder. In it were my beige suit (I was wearing the blue one), three blouses, a jumper, a pair of jeans, six pairs of underwear, two pairs of shoes, make-up, contact lens solutions, a computer chess set, and four novels, the names of which I still remember. That's the type of mind I have – events can merge and blur but the details remain, implacable. I'd change that, given the choice. I trust my memory with specifics but, when it comes to the wider picture, the older I get the less I know.

In my left hand was a small electronic typewriter. In my right was a maroon leather briefcase with Orion files and a days-old copy of *The Age* I'd been thrilled to find abandoned on a seat at the airport in Abu Dhabi. I carried that newspaper around for three weeks.

Walking through the glass sliding doors into the arrival hall, I felt like Alice going through the looking glass. Who, then, did that make Adam?

But Adam wasn't there. I laughed and shook my head. In fact, I didn't mind. I was savouring being here. Every place I'd been to in Asia and the Gulf, Steven had been there before. Schiphol would become *my* airport.

The Avis desk had an envelope with my name on it. Five

minutes later, I was in the left-hand side of a silver-blue Opel.
I started the ignition nervously. The other side of the world
was one thing, but the other side of the *road*? I'd never been
a particularly good driver even on my own side. But I could
see the Hilton Schiphol from where I was sitting, and I gently
released the handbrake.

In the muted golds and browns of the lobby, sixty people,
perhaps more, slumped in couches and on the floor, with
suitcases at their feet. Nobody moved.

"Charter flight," said the desk clerk, by way of explanation.
"Delayed."

"Laurie Michaels," I said. "Arrived."

He consulted a register. "Orion Management Systems. Mr
Sarris stays with us quite often."

"He's my boss."

The man looked at the register again and smiled. "Someone
made a mistake. It's written here, three months. You must
want a room for three days."

"No, three months is correct."

"You want to stay here for *three months*?"

"Is it possible to have a room overlooking the runways?"

"You want a room overlooking the *runways*?"

"Do you repeat everything?"

"My name's Felix," he said, extending his hand. "I don't
often bother to introduce myself. People usually stay for one
night. Could you fill in these forms?"

After we'd shaken hands and I'd given him my passport,
he said: "Do you mind if I ask you? Why you decided to stay
here? Instead of near your office?"

"It will be convenient. I'll be travelling a lot." I gave Felix
the finished forms and he returned my passport with another
smile.

"What the hell," I said. "I'll tell you the truth. I've always wanted to live in an airport."

My room on the fourth floor did, indeed, overlook the runways. A KLM jet was readying for takeoff when I walked in. I watched, through the heavily glazed window. There was no sound. The aircraft shimmered in the morning light. It didn't look real. Again, I thought of Alice, and of Susan.

I turned on the radio to acclimatise myself to the sounds of a new language; put clothes in the cupboard, books by the bed, and ran a bath. It was not yet 8.30 a.m. Another plane gathered speed along the runway then lifted off, outside the frame of my window.

Adam had left a sketch map for me at reception, together with a message that he and Frans, his second-in-charge, would return to the office from Düsseldorf that afternoon. I followed the map to the office alongside farmland, greenhouses, wind-mills and canals. The light was grey-blue, much softer than in Asia. Houses, fences, grass and trees were pastel-coloured, subtle, relaxed, a far cry from the assault of primary colours I'd been used to closer to the Equator.

I turned off the highway at the exit before the one to Gouda, as Adam had indicated on the map, and I tried to loosen the knot of disappointment that had formed in my chest.

The road led to an industrial estate of long, low, grey buildings. Surrounding the estate were dairy farms. The smell of cow dung was strong, even from the highway. There were no apartments or shops or cafes, only these low concrete buildings and aprons of car parks.

The block that housed Orion was at the end of the estate. All the famous computer names were here, on smart directory boards at the entrance and inside, by the lifts. The interior was as hi-tech as the companies represented. It's a look I like, but where was there to *walk*? Where was there somewhere to have coffee? I was an Australian in Europe, and this was not my idea of what Europe would be.

The familiar glass doors with the silver Orion logo were on the second floor. A woman with blonde eyebrows and freckles on her nose greeted me from behind a curved silver-painted desk. "*Goedemorgen*," she said.

"*Goedemorgen*," I replied. "I'm afraid that's all the Dutch I know. You must be Annelies."

She stood and extended her hand. "And you must be Laurie. We've been expecting you. Let me show you around."

I followed her down a long narrow corridor, its silver-painted walls reflecting us as we walked. To the left was a presentation and training room, and a large open-plan office area. To the right was a kitchen, followed by small offices for the financial controller and the sales executives, then interconnecting suites for Adam Sarris and Frans Timmerman, the man Adam had hired as his deputy, about whom Steven had declined to comment when I'd asked. In the small space that connected the suites was a desk for Ellen, Frans's and Adam's secretary.

Ellen was at the dentist's, Annelies said; and only Bart Kors, the financial controller, and Brian Sedgwick, the support manager, were in the office.

Bart Kors nodded politely when Annelies introduced me, but was eager to return to his computer screen.

Brian Sedgwick was more friendly. "Pull up a chair," he said, as Annelies smiled and disappeared into the corridor.

Brian was a small, dark, neat man with slightly pointed ears. His desk, in the corner of the room, had an orderly arrangement of perspex trays and coloured pens. There were seven other desks. I took a chair from the one closest to us.

"You don't sound Dutch," I said.

"Adam pulled me out of head office in London three months ago," he said. He widened his eyes in fair imitation of how Adam looked when trying to persuade. " 'Fancy the excitement of working in Holland?' Adam asked me. 'Super,' I said, thinking of the Prinsengracht and the Leidseplein. And then I found myself *here*." Brian gestured towards the window, with its panorama of highway and cows.

"Why do people put up with being here?"

"They love it," he said. "It's so spacious! So well-designed! So easy to park your car!"

"True," I said, and we both laughed. "Where is everybody?"

"Ah," said Brian. "The support consultants are on the road. But the sales offices yonder – " He pointed. "Are empty."

"Empty?"

Brian leaned forward across his desk. "Frans Timmerman," he said ominously.

"Frans doesn't seem terribly good at playing the popularity stakes," I said.

Brian inched forward a bit more. "What have you heard?"

"Nothing. That's the point. Whenever his name has come up the past couple of weeks – with Dick Staunton, Christopher Kendall, Steven Reid – there's a sort of choked silence."

"Frans came in as sales director only three weeks ago," Brian said. "Already, it seems like for ever. The first day he was here, he fired the two Dutch sales execs. He also fired the sales execs in Belgium, Germany, Austria, Switzerland and Italy. None of them had been with Orion for more than three months, so he was able to get rid of them during the probationary period. He wasn't prepared to give any of them a chance."

"Why not?"

Brian shrugged. "Clean sweep, I suppose. He's bringing in all the sales execs who worked for him at Mainline Systems, before Adam brought him into Orion. It's been one hell of a shock. He also tried to fire the sales execs in France, Sweden and Norway, but the general managers there threatened to resign and Adam intervened. Oh, and Angela Dennis, the training manager Adam hired from London, went home after a week."

"Why?"

"Frans. You look shocked."

"I am."

"So were we."

"But why did Adam allow it?"

"Ah," said Brian again. "Frans was Adam's first boss. He hired Adam as a rep in the London office of a Dutch technical instruments company where Frans was sent to be UK sales manager. Adam worked for him for years. He left the company when Frans quit to return to Holland, where he set up the European offshoot of Mainline Systems. Adam had a couple of other jobs before joining the time-share computer company where he met Jonathan and Ted."

"That *is* ancient history."

"Frans is ancient history himself. He's sixty."

"That would make him the oldest person in Orion."

"I dare say." Brian picked up a pen and twisted it between his thumb and forefinger. "Adam brought Frans here to work for him but, when you see them together, it looks the other way round."

"Mm," I said, wondering why I'd been hit by a sudden wave of tiredness. Orion people didn't get jetlag.

"Frans won't be pleased to see you," Brian said. "He's already had to get rid of Angela. That, as I told you, took him only a week." He stood up. "Let's get some coffee from the kitchen. It will be good to have you around. Adam says you left your mark in Asia."

"It will be harder to leave my mark here, I expect. It's technologically so much more sophisticated."

Brian laughed. We both looked out the window at the cows.

Angela Dennis's old desk was next to the window, across the room from Brian. In the top right-hand drawer was a set of Orion Constellation training manuals and a European restaurant guide. The bottom left-hand drawer contained a dozen tins of boiled sweets. On the window ledge was an ailing plant.

"Would you like a boiled sweet?" I asked.

"Not you, too! Angela was mad on boiled sweets."

At twelve thirty Annelies asked what type of sandwiches we wanted for lunch. We both ordered salad rolls, delivered half an hour later by bicycle from Gouda.

After lunch, Brian went to visit a client. I cleaned the desk, put my files away, watered the plant, and thought about what I'd say to Adam. I also thought about Steven, although I tried not to.

He picked up the phone immediately. "Steven Reid."

"Hi."

"Hi." His voice was cold.

"I just wanted to see how you were."

"I'm fine. Gotta run. Catch you later. Bye."

I was left in an empty office with several thousand miles of silence and, for an uncomfortable moment that seemed like a very long time, I felt I wasn't anywhere at all.

When Adam and Frans finally arrived, it was well past six. Frans did not shake my hand when I extended it after Adam had introduced us. Instead, he bent down and kissed my fingers. Then he looked me up and down, twice.

"Adam didn't tell me you were such a beautiful young lady," he said, looking at me with pale blue eyes, enlarged by perspex-framed spectacles beneath a thick white fringe.

I wanted to say something like "It's track record, not looks, that counts in a business relationship," but Adam's presence stopped me. "How kind of you to say so," I said.

"And where did you buy that charming beige suit?"

"Hong Kong," I said. "Where did you buy yours?"

This took Frans by surprise. "Men don't usually get asked that," he said.

"Perhaps that's because – " I said, then changed my mind. "Perhaps that's because men like to keep the secrets of their tailors to themselves."

Frans smiled at me with nicotine-stained teeth and fleshy cheeks. The smile was more a leer of triumph. I felt nauseous. Were all interactions with Frans going to be like this?

"We should have dinner," he said, "the three of us."

"Super," said Adam, and so I could hardly refuse. Nor could I refuse the door Frans held open of the silver Mercedes that he ushered me into, or the elaborate adjustments he made to the seat before deeming it fit for me to sit on.

Adam got in the back, and Frans started the car. "We'll go to Delft," he said. "I know a restaurant there."

Adam leaned forward, poking his head between Frans and me like an excitable puppy; like Steven, in fact. "You're going to *love* Holland," he said.

The restaurant was called *Het Straatje de Vermeer*.

"It means The Little Street of Vermeer," Frans told me. "Vermeer was a great painter."

I clenched my jaw.

Frans ordered a Scotch each for Adam and himself. "Would you like a glass of wine?" he asked.

"I'll have a mineral water, please," I said.

"You must have something stronger than that! We're celebrating your arrival."

"A mineral water will be fine."

The wine waiter hovered.

"That's not much fun," said Frans. "Join us in a Scotch, at least."

"That's kind of you, but no. I'll have a mineral water."

Frans turned to the waiter at last. "And a mineral water for the young lady," he said.

The waiter nodded and left. Frans said: "What are you afraid of?"

"I'm not afraid of anything," I said, and then: "I don't hold my drink too well." This was not true, but it seemed the easiest way of defusing the tension that Frans had insisted on creating. "Some women are like that."

The words had the desired effect. "It's good for a young lady to know her limitations," Frans said. "There's nothing worse than seeing a young lady drunk. Now, I suggest we all order the venison. It's very good here."

"Super," said Adam.

I looked longingly at things on the menu I would have preferred. "That's fine by me," I said.

Frans leaned back and lit a cigar. "Tell me about yourself," he said, with another show of stained teeth.

"I met Adam in Hong Kong," I began.

"You've got to understand that this is a new world for me," Frans said. "When I was a young man, women didn't have careers. Although it was different during the war, of course. In those days, *everyone* had to work. In fact, some of the most capable people I dealt with during the war were women."

Clearly, this was a prelude to anecdote. In some ways I was relieved. I had no burning desire to tell Frans "about myself" – whatever would I say?

"I spent most of the war in the Resistance," Frans continued, "even though I was only a teenager. There was a lady radio operator in the Resistance whose technical knowledge was every bit as good as mine. She also had the most marvellous legs, and we had the most passionate affair. What it was to be young!"

"Tell Laurie about the time you sabotaged the German General's car," said Adam.

Frans inhaled deeply on his cigar. "Now that's *some* story," he said. "We were *some* people."

The venison arrived mid-tale. Adam and I listened while we ate. Frans managed to eat as well, in between chunks of narrative.

"To this day," he concluded, "the Germans still don't know why that car blew up. The General was killed, and two other officers. What about some port and cheese?"

"Super," said Adam.

"I'd like a cup of tea," I said.

Frans motioned for the waiter and ordered. "After the war," he said, addressing himself mainly to me, "there was much rebuilding to be done. I don't just mean the cities and the industries. People's spirits had to be rebuilt, too. The younger generation don't understand how much that took."

After the meal, Frans drove us back to the office, where I'd left the car.

Adam transferred his bags from the Mercedes to the Opel, and Frans kissed my hand. "It's been a pleasure having dinner with a woman who has so much to say for herself," he said.

I looked at his fleshy face and wondered if he was being

ironic. I decided he wasn't, which was even worse. "See you tomorrow," I said.

"Not tomorrow, no. I'm going to Brussels in the morning."

Adam got into the driver's seat of my car, and I walked around to the passenger's side.

"He was really impressed with you," Adam said while reversing the car. "He's going to do great things for Orion out here. I only wish I could get the guys in Paris, Stockholm and Oslo to see that. They've formed a sort of alliance against him and I don't understand why. He's got more sales know-how in his little finger than they've got in . . ."

It had been a long day, with a lot to absorb, and I dozed in and out of sleep, snapping alert again when Adam mentioned Steve.

"He's been trying to get Howard to agree on a compromise figure for weeks, but Howard's been holding out for the whole amount."

"Howard?" I asked.

"Howard Crann. Excuse me, Howard G. Crann. The Texan. Sydney."

"Of course." Sydney seemed so far away.

"Since the oil slump, the property market in Houston has fallen through the floor. Steven suggested that Howard hold on to his house there awhile but Howard refused. Apparently he's already bought some over-the-top place in Elizabeth Bay. And then, yesterday, Steven got a telex from Jonathan. It said: 'Sort it out or I'll find a manager who can.' Steven was *ropable*. Can't say I blame him."

"Do you think Jonathan meant it?"

"If I were Steven, I wouldn't want to find out. Jonathan has been so – " Adam seemed to be searching for the right word – "so *aggressive* since Christmas. And, I don't know –

all this talk about Orion Constellation II being released next year."

My sleepiness vanished. "What happened at Christmas?" I asked, trying to sound casual. "And what's Orion Constellation II?"

But Adam had turned into the Hilton car park. "Well," he said, "here we are. Welcome aboard. Tomorrow we'll talk marketing strategy. It's going to be a great year. For both of us."

"Adam, I'm here for *three months*."

"You can't seriously be thinking of trading all this – " the sweep of his hand took in the airport – "for a classroom at Princeton?"

"Columbia."

Adam got out of the car, opened the back door, and reached for his luggage.

"Adam," I said, "I don't think you're *listening*."

Adam stared at me, his suit-carrier slung over his right shoulder, and his briefcase in his left hand. "Amazing," he said. "Sometimes you sound just like Della."

The telephone woke me from what seemed like a stupor. I had difficulty reaching across for the receiver.

"Hi," said Adam, "I thought we could discuss marketing strategy."

I looked at the clock beside the bed. "At 6.02 a.m?"

"In fifteen minutes, over breakfast. Frans wants me to go to Brussels with him. We could have a couple of hours together before he picks me up."

Downstairs, in the Dutch Oven restaurant, Adam was reading yesterday's *Financial Times* and *International Herald Tribune*, seemingly both at once, and eating a huge open sandwich of ham and cheese on rye.

"Best cheese in Europe," he said, motioning me to sit down. I did and he waved the *FT* at me. "Steven told me to put everything into stock in Japan. I didn't. I should have. He must have made a packet last week. What do you want to eat?"

I helped myself to yoghurt and fruit from the buffet. Adam read my two-page marketing proposal.

"This looks reasonable," he said.

"Of course it's reasonable. *I'm* reasonable."

Adam smiled. "Now, then, I didn't say *that*!"

"Once the blueprint is in place," I said, "we'll need a marketing person in each country."

"We've already got a marketing guy in Paris," Adam said. "Jean-Claude somebody. He was hired by the general manager there. And we've got someone in Düsseldorf, who was hired by the sales manager for Germany. I mean, the *former* sales manager for Germany."

"Was this the sales manager who was . . . who, uh, left when Frans joined Orion?"

"Frans fired him. How did you know? Frans wanted to fire the marketing person there, too, but there was some problem with the contract. Her name's Marthe."

"I see."

"Marthe Gerstmann. It's spelt M-a-r-t-h-e but it's pronounced like martyr. What do you mean, *I see*?"

"Has Frans ever chosen to have a woman work for him?"

"Of course he has. He even brought Ellen with him from Mainline Systems. He says she's the best secretary in Holland. Why are you looking at me like that? Oh, I see your point." Adam motioned for some coffee. "Frans is from another era.

You've got to remember that. I thought you Aussies were famous for giving people a go."

"So we'll be recruiting people for Belgium, Spain, Sweden, Norway, Denmark, Italy . . ."

"Possibly Greece and Turkey."

"And someone to replace me."

"Get some headhunters to handle it. But maybe you'll change your mind." He smiled and I smiled too.

"Perhaps I should go to London and Houston," I said. "See what the marketing departments have that we'd be able to use."

"Sure," he said, "but don't hold your breath. There are lots of glossy brochures with pretty pictures, but the words don't amount to much. There's all this stuff coming out of the States about *Reach for the stars – reach for Orion*, but it doesn't tell you what Orion Constellation actually *does*. Maybe that works over there – though I doubt it – but there's no point giving that sort of stuff to the Germans, for example." He stared gloomily at the tablecloth. "They want chapter and verse, in the most technical way possible. They want to know more than Max James does, and he *invented* Orion Constellation.

"Frans and I are running around Europe giving presentations, and we don't have any decent brochures in the relevant languages. Languages are the *least* of it. We don't have anything suitable to translate in the first place. Jonathan says, *Where are the sales*? But it's different out here. You can't sell in Europe with slogans and colour pictures. Jonathan doesn't understand that."

Adam opened his briefcase and pulled out a memo from Jonathan to Adam, Steven, and the managing directors of Britain and North America. It said: "All stops must be pulled out to maximise revenue flow and profits for this fiscal year. Repeat, all stops by May 31."

"That's less than a week away," I said.

"You're telling *me*," he said glumly. "Hence the trip to Brussels. Belgian Telecommunications are about to be offered prices the likes of which will not be seen again. It's a case of never mind the margin, look at the gross." He paused. "We can increase book-entry profit by discounting a couple of items," he said, more to himself than to me. "We can call them demonstration models."

Adam was quiet a few moments.

"I suppose next year will be easier," I said.

"Why do you say that?"

"Isn't Orion Constellation II due for release next year?"

"Who told you that?"

"You did. Yesterday."

"Oh," said Adam. "Well, it's no big deal. Just R and D. Max James is working on improvements, at the R and D place in Scotland."

"What sort of place is it?"

Adam relaxed. "It's a castle, would you believe!"

"Orion Constellation is being improved all the time," I said, "so I take it that Orion II is a completely new version?"

Adam's guardedness returned. "You know how it is – computer wizards always want to come up with some new wizardry."

"Perhaps I could go to Scotland and write a short article on what's going on there – for the Orion magazine," I said. "I might even be able to sell it elsewhere."

Adam looked at me sharply. "You don't have time to go to Scotland. And next fiscal year is going to be harder, not easier."

"Why?"

Adam pointed at the door. "There's Frans," he said, waving his *FT*. "You had a honeymoon in Asia, you know – apart from the obvious, I mean. The next few months are going to be make or break, the next few months are going to be *serious*."

The marketing executives in the London office were polite, but they answered questions as briefly as possible and volunteered nothing. "We assumed someone from here would get your job," one of them said after too many beers at lunch.

The reception in Houston was heartier. The marketing manager met me at the airport in a business suit teamed with cowboy boots and belt. (The hat was in the car.) At the office, a grey glass structure with an atrium full of plants, I was inundated with research reports, brochures, advertising campaigns, outlines of conferences and seminars. A three-day programme had been prepared.

The schedule also included window-shopping at the Galleria, house-ogling in River Oaks, and a barbecue in my honour at the marketing manager's house. The chatter was non-stop. People asked about Australia, and repeated what Howard G. Crann had told them on the phone from Sydney. They asked about Europe. But most of all they asked about Asia. "Steven, the amazing Steven!" they'd say, several times a day, everyone from the manager to the receptionist.

"I'm at the Sheraton Town and Country."

"Can't talk," said Steven from Singapore. "I'll ring you tomorrow."

"Hi."

"I'm in a meeting. I'll call you tomorrow."

"That's what you said yesterday." These words shocked me, with their whine and reproach. They did not fit the type of woman I wanted to be.

"Don't pressure me," Steven said. "I'm under enough pressure already. Jonathan's giving us hell."

"So Adam tells me."

"What does Adam tell you?" he asked harshly.

"That Jonathan said to pull out all stops."

"What *else* does Adam tell you?"

"Nothing much," I said, wary now. "He's hyped up about Europe, says it's poised to take off. Things like that."

"I hope Adam knows when to keep his mouth shut," Steven said.

I pulled the receiver away from my ear and looked at it stupidly for a moment before putting it back. "I beg your pardon?"

"You heard me."

I pulled the receiver away again and slammed it down.

Steven called back immediately. "How *dare* you hang up on me!"

"And how dare *you* treat me as the only person in your universe you don't have to charm! Your *ambivalence*. Your *nastiness*. I've had *enough*." And I slammed down the receiver for the second time.

As I stepped out from the office on to the landing at the top of the atrium, the explosion of greenery reminded me so much of Singapore that I almost lost my balance. I picked up my briefcase and walked down the stairs.

On the daunting, endless freeway, in the rent-a-car that was too big for me to handle comfortably, I tried to keep my hands and arms steady enough to drive. Turn-offs whizzed by. Which was the right one? Where was I?

It took me two hours to find the Sheraton.

The phone was ringing when I opened the door to my room.

"Where have you been?" asked Steven. "The office told me you were going back to the hotel. I've been ringing every ten minutes. I've been worried sick. Are you all right?"

I stared at the cheery red wallpaper and the little folded sign on the coffee table saying to have a nice day. My neck and arms were drenched in sweat. "No," I said, "I'm not all right. I've never seen so many freeway lanes and exits and cross-overs in all my life."

"Los Angeles is worse," said Steven.

"I don't care about Los Angeles," I said and started to cry.

There was an embarrassed silence on the other end of the line. "You know how hard it is for me to say sorry," Steven said. He swallowed noisily. "I'm sorry."

"Sorry doesn't make everything all right!" I wailed. But something significant had happened, at last. "I really don't ask for much," I said, wincing at the self-righteousness of my tone. "Just an occasional telephone call."

"It's difficult to co-ordinate times."

"You spend most of your life co-ordinating telephone times."

There was another embarrassed silence. "I don't know what you want me to say."

"I don't want you to say anything."

"I'll be in Houston next week."

"If I'd known that," I sighed, "I would have delayed my departure. I fly back to Holland day after tomorrow."

"I only just found out myself. Jonathan wants to finalise the figures for the year, before the executive committee meeting in Amsterdam in a couple of weeks. There'll be blood on the walls. Some of it will be mine."

I stretched out on the bed and closed my eyes. "I wish I could help."

"You do. I'll ring you tomorrow. That's a promise."

I put down the receiver – gently this time – and fell into an exhausted sleep. An hour later, I was woken by a phone call from the lobby, and had no time to do anything other than comb my hair before going downstairs for an office dinner I'd completely forgotten.

chapter nine

When I flew into Schiphol, I could see my room from the plane, and I wondered if there was a woman in the hotel watching the runways, as I liked to do, and if we'd meet — over breakfast perhaps or late at night in the bar.

After I'd unpacked, the phone rang. A delighted, inebriated Steven said: "We made budget! Graham signed a multi-system deal in Sumatra!"

"How did he do that?"

"He said it was better I didn't ask, so I didn't ask." Which I interpreted to mean that Steven didn't want to tell me.

In the morning, I read *The Guardian* and the *International Herald Tribune* in the restaurant downstairs. There were quite a few men on their own, but no women.

There were no women sitting alone the following morning, either, or the morning after that. I became friendly with one of the waitresses, who brought photographs of her daughter and her house. The photographs jolted me. They were post-cards from real life.

At the office, I prepared a proposed marketing strategy for Europe, my desk piled high with documents from London and Houston. I tried to arrange a meeting with Adam.

"Sure," he'd say, "right now. I just need to make a couple of calls."

Later, he'd put his head around the door to my office and say: "I have to go to Paris. The French take no notice of what you say on the phone." Or: "I have to go to Oslo." Or Copenhagen. Or Milan.

"Lucy," I said on the phone, "I'm going mad! I have to get my marketing strategy approved but Adam seems to have developed an allergy to meetings."

Lucy laughed. "If Adam won't come to a meeting," she said, "take the meeting to him."

"That's brilliant," I said. "I miss you."

"I miss you, too." There was a pause. "Things have changed."

"In what way?"

"Steven seems, well, *hesitant*. About everything. And Graham – Graham made a string of premature sales in Sumatra, and now Ian finds himself having to provide support to planning engineers who can hardly *read*, let alone input data. I'm not enjoying it out here any more. But that's enough of me. How's Holland? Will you send me a copy of your strategy?"

"Of course. I'd welcome your comments."

That night, driving in soft dusk back to the hotel, a barge steamed alongside in the canal, bicycles swished past, and herons glided overhead. I wished there had been someone with me, to share the beauty of the scene. The thought surprised me. Sharing a scene had never seemed to matter much before.

Annelies buzzed me, as I'd asked her to do, as soon as Adam and Frans arrived. I grabbed the file at the edge of my desk and rushed into the corridor.

"Hi!" said Adam, with the extravagant smile that always made me glad to see him, however exasperated I may have had reason to be. Frans nodded curtly and went into his room. I followed Adam into the office adjoining.

"I recognise that look," he said, hanging up what I secretly thought of as his Famous Blue Raincoat. "Della gets that look from time to time."

"Marketing strategy," I said, smiling and waving the file. "Recommendations therein. Approval necessary. Discussion required."

"Discussion granted. Preliminaries dispensed. Start now. Do not pass Go."

"You can send me up all you like," I laughed. "So long as I've got your attention, I don't care."

Adam laughed, too. The telephone buzzed and I heard Ellen say: "Dick Staunton, Riyadh."

After he'd finished the conversation with Dick, the receiver was in its cradle barely a minute before Christopher Kendall was on the other line from Abu Dhabi. ("Do Dick and Christopher let each other know when they've tracked Adam down?" I asked Lucy Phillips later. "Of course," she said. "Have you only just worked that out?")

After Dick's call, Adam said: "I'm all yours."

I opened the file. Frans walked in.

"Adam," he said, "we must discuss Werner Construction."

"Frans," I said, "I've been waiting more than a week. All I want is half an hour."

Frans looked at Adam before looking at me. "Pushy women don't generally do well in Europe," he said and walked out.

"Do you mind if we schedule this later?" Adam asked, shifting about in his chair. "I really should talk to Frans." He paused. "Frans taught me everything I know. It wasn't easy getting him to come and work for me. I had to persuade Jonathan to let Frans buy shares – rather more shares than Jonathan might have liked. Some other people weren't too pleased about it, either. Steven, for example."

I returned to my desk and opened a book I'd bought at the

airport news stand the night before. The book was called *Get Set For Corporate Success*. On page five was this paragraph: "Effective managers have their lives under control. They know who they are, what they want, and how not to get sidetracked. Effective managers don't have messy personal lives which prevent them from concentrating. Before you read on, sort out your life."

I started laughing and almost choked on one of Angela's boiled sweets.

"Are you all right?" asked Brian.

"Let me read you this paragraph," I said. I did. He didn't respond. "Don't you think that's funny?"

"It's pretty self-evident, I would have thought," he said. "Not something to give rise to laughter."

"Not laughter as in light-hearted, funny," I said with a sharp, painful yearning for Susan – the old Susan. "Laughter in the dark."

Brian looked at me warily, then shifted his gaze to the door. Adam was standing there, with the Famous Blue Raincoat slung across one shoulder. "I'm sorry," he said, "truly I am, but I've got to catch the four o'clock to London."

"I'll drive you to the airport," I said, grabbing the file, my handbag, and the tin of boiled sweets.

"Fine," he said, "I'll tell Ellen to cancel the taxi."

It would take thirty-five minutes to drive to the airport: thirty-five minutes without Ellen or Frans; thirty-five minutes without telephone, telex or fax; thirty-five minutes of Adam to myself.

As it turned out, I had Adam for almost an hour and a half because the flight was delayed. In a quiet, comfortable corner of the KLM lounge, the marketing plan got approved.

When I returned to the hotel, I felt enthusiastic and chatty, but there was no one to be enthusiastic or chatty *with*, except perhaps for Felix, but he wasn't on duty.

It was too early to ring Lucy in Singapore, and I didn't feel like another awkward night of dinner with a stranger in the restaurant downstairs. I ordered room service and turned on the TV.

Octopussy was half-way through. Again. *Octopussy* alternated with *Raiders of the Lost Ark* that month on the Hilton Schiphol's closed circuit TV. I never saw either film from beginning to end – just fragments of them, sequences which merged together and became a bizarre parallel life.

Jean-Claude Mabire adjusted his cravat. "Your marketing plan is very interesting," he said. "Now I will tell you mine."

When he'd finished, I said: "That is totally different."

"*La France*," he said solemnly, "is totally different."

I looked around at the pink velvet couches and the silver scalloped drapes. Adam always referred to the Paris office as The Boudoir. When *La France* had failed to make budget the previous quarter, Adam had said: "It's the décor. They're all asleep there."

"We're going to have to work together," I said.

"*Mais oui*," he said cheerfully, clearly intending nothing of the kind.

But I wasn't overly concerned. Jean-Claude Mabire was conscientious and astute, and France was, as he said, a country apart. Adam agreed that Jean-Claude should be given a free hand. "Within reason," he said. "That is, if you think you can reason with the French."

Düsseldorf was a different matter. Marthe Gerstmann had a permanent scowl and shoulders braced as though for assault.

She weighed all suggestions carefully and was detailed in her explanations of why none of them would work.

Oslo, Stockholm and Copenhagen, by contrast, were models of co-operation and efficiency. "You've done a good job there," Adam said in the car one morning from the airport to the office, after I'd waited for his flight from Sweden.

"I can hardly take credit for what's coming out of Scandinavia," I said.

"What are you talking about? You chose the people and you briefed them. That's what management *is*."

"I thought management was sorting out your life."

Adam glanced at me sideways. "I don't think I'd score too well, if that was the case," he said. He was silent for a few moments. "What about your replacement? What's happening with that?"

"I'm waiting on a shortlist from ExecuSearch."

"To be honest," he said, "I'm not so keen on companies like ExecuSearch. They present you with people who know how to write a CV rather than with people who can actually do the work. Is there anyone already in Orion, do you think, who would be suitable?"

Before I'd had a chance to reply, he said: "Do you think Steven plays his cards too close to his chest?"

"In relation to what?"

"In general."

"Why?"

Adam laughed. "You're becoming as cagey as he is." He stared at the road. "I think he's doing OK," he said, more to himself than to me. "What will you do after Princeton?"

"Columbia. I haven't thought that far ahead. I suppose I'll go back to Hong Kong." I paused in surprise; I hadn't known I was going to say that. "Assuming I'm still with Steven and if Steven's still there. Do you think he'll still be there?"

"He's doing OK," Adam said again. "That's not to say he hasn't needed defending at times. A few years back, when I suggested sending him to Saudi, people said: 'But he's too arrogant, too much of a smartarse.'" Adam scratched the back of his head. "Steven's done better than everyone thought he'd do – better than I thought he'd do. But I hope he doesn't have unrealistic expectations. It's going to be a case of toughing it out."

"Toughing what out?"

But we'd arrived at the office and Adam was already getting out of the car.

"*Lucy?*" Adam echoed in the KLM lounge at Schiphol the next day.

"She understands Orion," I said, looking at my watch to see how much time I had before Adam's flight was due to leave. My life had become as geared to Adam's flight schedules as it had been in Asia to Steven's. "She knows the client base. She knows the target industries."

"But she's a trainer."

"She *started* as a trainer. Steven's got her doing absolutely everything in Singapore. The alternative, if you're not happy with any of the candidates found by ExecuSearch, is to keep tabs on marketing yourself until you find a manager you *are* happy with."

"No," said Adam, "we need someone now. Would Lucy be interested, do you think?"

"She's keen to get back to Europe."

"Have you talked to her about it?"

"No."

"Could be worth a try."

"I'll talk to Steven," I said.

Adam tapped the handle of his briefcase. "No, find out if Lucy's interested. There's no point getting Steven involved if Lucy isn't even interested."

"I think I should speak to Steven first, in case he minds."

"You don't work for Steven," Adam said abruptly, "you work for me. He'll be here in a few days for the executive committee meeting. If Lucy agrees, we can talk about it then. If she isn't interested, there's no point bringing it up. As to whether Steven minds or not – that's beside the point. He's got to learn to think in terms of the company as a whole. In any case, Steven has always hired staff from wherever, and whomever, he pleased. Do you think Lucy could do the job?"

"In the short term, yes."

"Then talk to her."

Adam's flight was called and he stood up, slinging the raincoat across his shoulder.

I drove back to the Hilton, my chest as tight as my grip on the wheel. But I'd made a *business* suggestion, that's all, based on business criteria. Steven, however, wasn't going to see it like that.

In my room, I stood by the window, watched the planes, and decided to let the matter of Lucy lapse. Adam's mind would alight on other things, and chances were that if I did not bring it up again neither would he.

I should have gone out. Instead, I ordered room service and so was there for the call.

"Hi," said Lucy, "thanks for sending me your strategy. Things are really going to happen there. Do you think I'd be able to play a part?"

"Did you speak to Adam today, by any chance?"

"Adam? I haven't spoken to Adam in weeks. You're the only one who gets to speak to Adam."

"What did you have in mind?" I asked, unsure what to do.

"Could there be a slot for me in Europe?"

"What about Singapore?"

"Everything's in place here now. To be honest, I'm bored. And Ian – well, the situation with Ian is delicate. He's not cut out to be a manager. Would there be room for him in Holland?"

"He'd have to ask Brian. Are you serious about this?"

"Yes."

"Do you think you'd be able to take over from me?"

Lucy was silent. I waited, full of unease. I'd mentioned it now; I could hardly unmention it.

"I was thinking of something along the lines of responsibility for Benelux," Lucy said. "But of course I'd want your job. Who wouldn't?"

I laughed.

"Oh, well, you know what I mean," she said. "If I'd been a journalist and had been accepted by Columbia, I'd go, too. Do you think Adam would agree?"

"It's possible. I'll talk to him."

"Oh Laurie, would you?"

I put down the phone gently. Well, then, Lucy had approached me.

She rang again, the next day. I was working on a presentation Jonathan had requested for the executive committee meeting.

"Graham seemed quite positive," Lucy said.

My mind was on what I'd been doing, and I didn't immediately register the significance of what Lucy had said.

"He was a bit annoyed at not having been consulted," she continued, "and said he'd be sorry to lose me, but that he wouldn't stand in my way."

"What?"

"He said he'd talk to Steven."

"*What?*"

"He said he'd talk to Steven."

"But *I* haven't had a chance to talk to Steven yet!"

Brian was watching me from the opposite end of the room. He pretended to be working but his ears were stiff as antennae.

"When did he say he'd talk to Steven?" I asked.

"Sometime today."

"Where *is* Steven?"

"Houston."

I looked at my watch. It was 4 p.m. in Holland, which meant it was 9 a.m. in Houston and 11 p.m. in Singapore. "Lucy – " I said. "Never mind. I'll talk to you later."

The receptionist at the Houston office said Steven was not there. Sheraton Town and Country reservations said he had checked out the day before.

Brian ceased pretending to work. I dialled Graham at home. There was no reply. I kept dialling, hoping to catch him the minute he walked in.

And then Steven rang.

"Hello spaniel," I said. Brian put down his pen.

"What's the point of flying business class if they put your bags in with economy? Held me up half an hour."

"Are you *here?*"

"Yup. At the Marriott."

"I thought you were arriving in two days' time."

"Surprise!"

"Steve – "

"Aren't you surprised?"

"I'm surprised."

"Aren't you pleased?"

"I'm pleased. And, uh, I've got a surprise for you, too."

"I don't think I like the sound of that."

I closed my eyes. I'd have to get this over with. "Lucy

wants to take over from me when I leave. We talked about it yesterday. I discussed it with Adam and tried to ring you but Lucy spoke to Graham before I was able to find out where you were and the whole thing snowballed."

"You're taking the piss out of me. You're having me on."

I didn't respond.

"I don't think this joke is very funny," he said.

"It's not a joke."

"What *is* it; then – an attempt to undermine me?"

"Of course not. I'm just trying to do my job. Nothing's been done yet. It's just an idea. Adam said there was no point talking to you or Graham – "

"Adam said that?"

" – before finding out if Lucy was interested."

"Have you finished?"

"Yes," I said, my eyes still closed.

"How dare you approach my staff!"

"As a matter of fact, she approached me."

"The principle's the same. You should have spoken to me first."

"If I'd spoken to you first, would you have let me discuss it with Lucy?"

"Absolutely not."

"My job is to get a marketing services network off the ground."

"I can't believe you're saying this."

"Lucy asked *me*. As it happens, I think she'd be good for the job and I think the job would be good for her. She isn't happy in Singapore."

"That's the first I'*ve* heard of it."

"Nothing has happened. It's only a suggestion."

Steven slammed down the phone.

I stared at the receiver in despair.

First, I rang Lucy. Yes, she said, she'd call Steve immediately, to explain what had happened.

Next, I rang Graham, who answered this time, and who paraphrased what Adam had said about needing to consider Orion as a whole.

Then I rang Adam in London, insisting to the secretary that he be interrupted. "Steven's being silly," he said. "You can't hold someone like Lucy down. Steven gets this way sometimes. If he wants to have it out with me – fine."

I put down the phone and huddled over my desk. It was six o'clock. Brian put on his jacket quietly, and tactfully went home.

I left the office, too. Driving along rural roads to reach the highway for Amsterdam, I passed neat farmhouses whose picture windows edged in lace filled me with longing.

Steven opened the door. He stared at me blankly then held out his arms. "Don't say anything," he said.

We undressed wordlessly and wordlessly made love. Afterwards, we drifted into sleep.

I woke first. The lines around Steven's mouth and eyes were deeper than I remembered, and they aroused in me a sharp sense of love that was almost like pain. I wondered if I'd ever be able to feel this strongly for anyone else, which made me realise I didn't believe I'd be given the chance to watch Steve age.

When he opened his eyes, he said: "The word that comes to mind is *betrayal*."

"I love you," I said. And then, speaking softly, with the barest bones of language I knew, I tried to mend the harm. It had been a case of confused loyalties, I said. I had tried to do the right thing – by the company, by Adam, by Lucy – but had ended crossing the one person I cared about. I hadn't set out to undermine, I hadn't –. I couldn't talk any more. I lowered my head.

Steven was silent a long time. "I don't know where my anger's gone," he said at last, "but it has. I think you should stay with the company. I think you should go into sales. Adam would give you the opportunity, I'm sure of it."

"*You* weren't prepared to give me the opportunity in Asia," I said quietly.

"Asia was different. But, even so, I'd probably handle that differently now."

"It's too late," I said. But I said it without reproach. I had reversed a defeat of what seemed like a long time ago. It was way after the event, and had no practical benefit, but I had wrested from all this grief and regret a small private victory.

Steven went into Adam's office the next morning and shut the door. Ellen had not yet arrived, and I hovered around the photocopier near her desk. I could hear the anger in Steven's voice but he was talking too quietly for me to be able to make out the words. I returned to my desk and leafed through some material that Marthe Gerstmann had sent, more than a week late, from Düsseldorf.

Half an hour later, Adam buzzed my extension and asked me to come in. I put Marthe's papers aside and walked down the corridor.

Steven was talking to Ellen, explaining how he wanted a sales forecast document laid out. He did not look up.

Adam motioned for me to close the door. After I'd done so, he said: "The bugger chewed me out."

I did not speak.

"I guess he has a point," Adam said. "You really should have talked to him first. I explained that you didn't do it on purpose, that it was an oversight – inexperience, something like that."

I kept my face impassive, but my arms stiffened in rage. The story had been reconstructed, and it would be this version that would be remembered by Adam, Steven, and everyone else in Orion who might hear it one day, in the office, or over a glass of port in a hotel bar. Through its retelling, this version would become "the truth", the Gospel According to the Boys.

"Let's try to put that behind us now," Adam said. "You've probably learned something. No real damage has been done."

"No real damage," I echoed, my voice so flat that Adam took the words to mean that I agreed with him.

Here it was, the pattern of my childhood all over again. But I didn't see that at the time. I couldn't understand my frustration and helplessness; I couldn't fathom my rage.

Lucy stayed in Singapore. Steven enlarged her area of responsibility, increased her salary, and got Jonathan to agree to let her buy shares in the company. And so the incident was left behind, except in Steven's mind, and mine.

Jonathan arrived from Houston with Ogden Burroughs. Roger Benham flew in from London, and Dick Staunton from Riyadh. There were also two men I hadn't met before, who had opened Orion offices in Lagos and São Paulo.

All day Tuesday, they sat around a table in a Marriott conference suite. The morning, no doubt, would have been spent on what Steven always called Discussions of the Bleeding Obvious. But, when he rang me at the office that afternoon, I could hear from the tone of his voice that the discussions had shifted to what he probably would have called More Bleeding Than Obvious, had he wanted to talk to me about them at all.

"Jonathan suggested you join us for a drink this evening before we go out to dinner," he said. "You could meet us in the Library Bar of the hotel at seven o'clock."

"With pleasure," I said. "Where are we going to dinner?"

"I don't think I explained properly. Jonathan's inviting you to have drinks with us. Dinner will be a working one, I'm afraid. You'll be able to join us for dinner on Thursday night. Do you mind being on your own this evening? Is that all right?"

"Of course," I said.

But it wasn't all right. Steven would be in Amsterdam only three more nights. I'd spent hardly any time with him. That would not have mattered so much had the episode of Lucy not still hung in the air so palpably despite – or perhaps because of – the fact that it hadn't been mentioned again.

If only, I thought, and then stopped. "If only" were words that losers used, Steven always said.

Adam, Jonathan and Roger looked very much at ease among the deep leather armchairs of the Library Bar, surrounded by photographs of sports heroes hung on timber-panelled walls. The room seemed to scream *Males Only*. It was snubbing me.

I walked towards the tables. As I made to sit down, Jonathan stood up. Adam and Roger, following Jonathan's lead, stood up too. I froze. Not so many months before, I would have been able to make light of this awkwardness with laughter or a tilt of my head. I no longer seemed capable of such touches. I'd turned into the type of woman, for heaven's sake, who ascribed feelings to *rooms*.

"Steven and the others are making phone calls," Jonathan said. "Or so they say. What would you like to drink?"

"A Perrier, please," I said, sinking into a hostile armchair.

"What sort of a drink is that?" Jonathan demanded. "Have a real drink."

"I'd prefer a Perrier," I said.

The drinks were brought – whisky for Jonathan, Adam and Roger; mineral water for me – and Roger raised his glass in a toast to Orion. When the *hear, hear*s had subsided, Roger turned to me and said: "When your time's up here, would you consider coming to London?"

Adam banged his glass on the table and some whisky spilled. "Don't you dare try pinching my staff," he said.

I stared at him, but his face held no irony. The significance of what he'd just said had eluded him completely, or so I thought.

"That's very flattering," I said to Roger, "but I'm, uh, going to Princeton."

Adam grimaced. "Columbia," he said.

"Until now," I told the executive committee on Wednesday afternoon in the suite at the Marriott, "Orion has been marketed in terms of Orion Constellation the product, rather than Orion Management Systems the company and its clients."

I relaxed. The presentation was going well. I'd been nervous about the talk; had spent the morning rehearsing it; and had bought a new outfit – a wildly impractical cream wool dress that would have to be drycleaned every time I wore it but which had caused Steven to stare at me that morning as if for the first time and say: "You look smashing."

"The situation is changing, to some extent," I said. "We run articles in the Orion magazine about clients using Orion Constellation on specific projects. We describe those projects and the applications that are being used to plan and monitor them.

"But we could do more along the same lines. We could create an advertising campaign, for example, which embraces a series of customer profiles, each advertisement comprising a striking photograph and a quotable quote.

"We could talk to journalists about some of the larger or more unusual projects where Orion Constellation is being used. Some of those projects could find their way into print, some of them with a mention of Orion.

"The most effective way to sell Orion the product and Orion the company has been, and will continue to be, in terms of the prestigious companies that are our clients."

I paused. Jonathan nodded. A fraction of a second later, the others in the room nodded, too, and I was able to put my despair over Steven to one side. The people in the room were listening to me. There was no guarantee that they would follow my suggestions, but being listened to was a pretty good start. It did not constitute power in any real sense, of course, but the calm assurance that was mine in that moment seemed like a glimpse of how power might feel.

"Another way of adding to Orion's credibility and lustre," I said, on a roll now, "would be to try to organise a feature article – in the London *Sunday Times*, say – on the research and development of Orion II. An in-depth piece looking at the people involved, as well as the technology. It has everything going for it, this story, from the Scottish castle headquarters to the charismatic figure of Max James."

Something had gone wrong. Adam was focusing his eyes on me as though they were lasers, and everyone in the room seemed to have stopped breathing.

"Well," said Jonathan, "that was extremely interesting."

No one moved.

"That was extremely interesting," Jonathan repeated. A waiter wheeled in a trolley of tea and cakes.

Tea was poured and everyone avoided my gaze, Steven most of all. Why was talk of R and D in Scotland off limits? What was going on there? Defence systems for the military? Secret work for MI5? Software solutions for the Man on the Moon? Why wasn't I allowed to go and see? Why wasn't anyone allowed to talk to Max James?

When Steven returned after another working dinner with The Boys, I said, in a shrill, exasperated voice that I knew he hated: "What is there in Scotland that everyone's trying to *hide*?"

He thought for a few seconds while he took off his shoes. "Nothing," he said finally, undoing his tie.

"Nothing," I repeated sarcastically and went into the bathroom to wash my face. When I came out, Steve was in bed, asleep. I turned off the light. Lying beside him, I felt further away than if he'd been on the other side of the world.

At work the next day, everything seemed slowed down and opaque. I drank coffee to kick-start my veins, which felt invaded by ice.

Back at the Marriott, I had a hot bath but, in my underwear afterwards, I felt colder than before. I ran my hands along my arms, to warm them.

"I'll turn down the air-conditioning a bit," Steven said, moving across the room while putting on a shirt. "Is that better?"

"Thank you," I said. "Which blouse should I wear?"

Steven looked down and pretended to concentrate on getting the buttons in their correct holes. "It would, ah, be awkward if you came along."

"But you said Thursday dinner would include me." I wished

I hadn't said that. I was tired of beginning sentences with "but". I was tired of sounding like a six-year-old.

"Yes, I know, but now Jonathan has arranged a tour of the bordellos."

"I didn't know anyone used that term any more."

"Bordello? Jonathan does."

On my arms, I felt the familiar prickly heat of the hated nervous rash. Soon my arms would swell.

"I'm just going to have a few drinks," he said. "I'm not going to take part in the rest of it. You know me better than that."

"That's not the point," I said. "It's tacky, but it's not the point. Let the boys play while they're away, if they must. That's not my business, that's not the point. The point is that I'm here with *you*."

"But I can't be the only one not there!"

"You're leaving tomorrow, and I've got an early flight to Paris."

"I'll get back as early as I can."

I watched him leave, and the chill got worse. But the air-conditioning was as low as it could go.

Outside, there was a warm summer breeze. It was the beginning of "the blue hour" – dusk – and, as I crossed the road in front of the hotel, the neon lights of the Leidseplein came into view. The tables and chairs in front of the cafes were animated with people smoking, drinking, and watching the passing parade. I hurried along the Leidsestraat and turned right, on to the Prinsengracht.

How beautiful this city was. The brick-paved street had been worn smooth by centuries of feet and bicycles. Behind curtainless windows, people sat and talked, the lights of their apartments bathing them in a warm and intimate glow.

Windows of houseboats were lit, too, and they cast golden

beams into the canal. Some green-billed ducks climbed out of the water on to a platform of logs beside one houseboat that had a floating garden. A woman leaned out of the boat's small kitchen and tossed the ducks some bread.

Gentle arcs of bridges reflected themselves in the still water of the canal. Everything was orderly and calm. The only source of agitation in the scene was me.

Homesickness and longing settled around my shoulders, and I had to lean against a streetlamp for a moment, to let the sadness ease. One day, perhaps, I'd return to Amsterdam under different circumstances and be able to blend in with the reflections of the canals. Right now, however, there was just homesickness and longing, and the realisation that I no longer even knew what I was homesick or longing *for*.

Sometimes — mercifully not often — you wake and for a moment don't know where in your life you are. Disparate people clamour. The child trying to please hard-to-please parents. The teenager with the mile-a-minute jokes. The newspaper woman, name on the front page. The business-woman, briefcase of regrets. None of it explicable. Or perhaps too easily so, with enough remembering of things gone to great lengths to forget. The things we never mention, except on the psychiatrist's couch, of which I'd always been wary. Dismantle our defences, Susan and I used to say, and there'll be nothing left to house who's home. I'm suspicious of people who, like me, traffic in repartee. We are ill-quipped for living.

"For God's sake, turn off the alarm!" said Steven.

I reached over, pushed down the button and stared at this pale, freckled man clutching a pillow to his head. What part of my life was this? Who was I trying to please? What had happened to the jokes?

"It's 6.30 a.m.," said Steven. "Why is the clock set for 6.30 a.m?"

"I have to be at Schiphol by eight."

"Oh." He let the pillow fall to one side. "I tried to wake you when I got in last night. You seemed drugged." He paused, as though he'd asked a question. Perhaps he had. I didn't respond. "You were right," he continued. "I shouldn't have gone. If it's any consolation, I had a lousy time. The others got drunk and made fools of themselves. Adam and I slunk off to a bar where we talked about Della and you."

Steven's words seemed indistinct, far away.

"Let's go to the Lake District," he said.

"I have to be in Paris. ExecuSearch has come up with six candidates there."

"So Adam told me. You can take an early evening flight to Manchester. I'll meet you at the airport. We'll reach Ambleside before the pubs close."

"When do the pubs close?"

"Eleven."

"That's driving too fast."

"You don't even know how far it is."

"It's not far that bothers me, it's *fast*."

Steven smiled. "I miss your witty comebacks," he said.

"No you don't."

"I do. Tuesday, we can drive to Newcastle. You can meet my parents."

"Your parents?"

"I do have them, you know."

"I wasn't disputing that."

"We can stay the night and fly to London Wednesday evening. Thursday morning, I'll go to Hong Kong and you can come back here."

"Adam won't let me take off a few days, just like that."

"Actually, he will. He agreed to, last night."

I could have said no, of course. But the story I was living, however much I disliked the direction of the plot, was too compelling.

"It's momentums like these – " I said, and got out of bed.

chapter ten

The flight from Paris to Manchester was delayed. Jean-Claude Mabire had driven like a madman through peak-hour traffic to get me to the airport despite my protestations that I could have gone by train.

The day had not been a success. Despite some formidable CVs, none of the candidates presented by ExecuSearch had been impressive. "I'm the obvious person for the job," Jean-Claude had said after we'd completed the interviews.

In fact, I agreed with him, but Jean-Claude had been excluded from consideration. "His loyalty would be to the Paris office, not to me," Adam had said.

The plane finally took off at a quarter to eight.

In the arrival hall at Manchester airport, Steven shifted his weight from one leg to the other and back again. "Isn't it great to be here!" he said, with his boyish manic grin. He gave me a hug. As he took my suit-carrier from my shoulder, a stranger's reflection in the window bathed Steven's face in a soft blue light.

Outside, in the darker blue of night, Steven put the suit-carrier on the back seat of a silver Mercedes.

"What's this?" I asked.

"A Mercedes-Benz."

"I can see that. What's it doing here?"

Steven shrugged and smiled. "I was standing at the Avis counter and, well, I said I'll take a Mercedes."

"Look at all these controls," he said, when we got in. "It's like a plane!"

We reached the pub at a quarter to eleven.

"Steven!" said a woman about my age sitting at a table near the bar. Her hair, cropped stylishly short, was the same colour as Steve's. She had green eyes, which she emphasised with green eyeshadow, green earrings, and a green knit dress. "We wondered what had happened to you," she said when we reached the table and sat down.

A few moments later we were joined by a dark, stocky man carrying two glasses of beer. "You've arrived, then, have you?" he said to Steven with a mock grimace. "I suppose you'll be expecting a beer as well?"

Steven laughed. "How are you, you old sod?"

"I told her you'd turn up," he said, motioning to the woman in green. "She's Rosemary, by the way," he said to me, "and I'm Nigel." He put down the beers. "You must be Laurie. If we waited around for the lad here to introduce us, we'd never know one another's names."

"Can't get a word in edgewise, is the problem," said Steven, laughing. "Where's my beer?"

"Be patient, lad," said Nigel. "I'm talking to Laurie. Your beer can wait."

"I'll get it myself, then!" Steven said, and stood up.

When he returned, with a beer for himself and a mineral water for me, his bowlegged walk seemed more pronounced than usual.

"The weather's been marvellous," Rosemary said to me. "We haven't had a summer like this in years. You'll be seeing the lakes at their absolute prettiest."

"The climbing's never been so good," Nigel said to Steve. "You won't believe it, the ground's *dry*."

"You're right," said Steve, "I don't believe it. The ground's never dry in the Lake District. That's the point of it!"

"He wouldn't know, would he!" Nigel said, winking at me. "He's never *here*. All this jetting around the world – I mean, where does it get you?"

"Around the world," Steve said, and they both laughed.

When we left the pub, Rosemary said: "Where did this Mercedes come from?" She walked up to it and inspected the Avis sticker. "Steven," she said, "you'll have to drive me shopping tomorrow morning, and to tennis in the afternoon. Then we can drive along the high street. Slowly."

Nigel didn't comment. "You'll follow us, then," he said.

We'd be staying with Rosemary and Nigel because Steven's house was rented out.

Steven had mentioned Nigel many times. They'd met on a rock climbing expedition during university, while Steven was studying engineering and Nigel, medicine. Nigel and Rosemary had met in a Manchester hospital some years later, when he was a registrar and she a medical student. They had returned to the Lake District, where each of them had grown up, and were now partners in two separate medical practices, at opposite ends of the high street. "We're Ambleside's medical parentheses," Nigel had said.

"I like them," I told Steven in the car.

"They're not at all pretentious, are they? They lead a very down-to-earth life."

"What do they make of your life?"

"They don't really know much about my life. They just accept that, every few months or so, I show up in Ambleside."

"What do they think about your work?"

"I never talk about work here."

"Why not?"

Steven shrugged and turned into the driveway of a large

stone, bay-windowed house. "We're here," he said. "Just smell the air!"

In the entrance hall, terracotta jugs held manicured miniature trees. There were plants on the coffee table and the window ledge in the sitting room. The curtains and the sofas were covered in a green-and-beige floral print.

I put down my suit-carrier. "You have a lovely home," I said.

"Thank you," said Rosemary. "Where are you living?"

"The Hilton. The Schiphol Hilton."

Rosemary laughed. "Sounds very high-powered. But where do you live?"

I suddenly felt tired and didn't know what to say.

Rosemary was embarrassed. "I mean, where do you keep your things?"

"In that bag," I said.

Rosemary looked uncertain then laughed. "You *Australians*!" she said.

Nigel and Steven came inside, after examining the finer points of the Mercedes. Steve and I took our bags to the guest room upstairs. When we came down, Rosemary walked in from the kitchen with tea and cakes on delicately patterned china that complemented the curtains and the couch.

I looked around the room slowly, taking pleasure in the cumulative effect of the objects in it, each of them carefully chosen and placed. It was a woman's room and it embraced me.

I stood in the bathroom next morning and applied conceal-ment make-up to the rash that had started on my arms at the Marriott and had spread to my shoulders and face.

"Are you all right?" asked Steven from the other side of the door. "What are you *doing* in there? Breakfast is getting cold."

We went walking. Steven showed me Ambleside, Windermere, Grasmere and Bowness, as though he'd created them. Each hill, each lake had a name – which he knew – and personal significance: the time he'd lost his footing on this particular rock; the time Nigel, after a beer-induced argument, had pushed him into that lake; the time when, alone in heavy rain, he'd stood among trees doing battle with the wind and had been overcome by joy.

For three days we walked and he held my hand. At night, he whispered "I love you". But there was something strained in how he said it. There was something strained, too, about his constant chatter and the way he touched my hair.

On Monday night, in bed, I said: "You're trying hard, I know, but love shouldn't have to be like that."

"You're right," he said. "It's just not there."

My skin burned beneath the make-up, like a hidden mark of shame. "It's a hard thing for me to accept," I said quietly.

"I haven't wanted to accept it, either," he said. "I've been living in the Now."

I looked up at the ceiling, with its restored cornices, and then at the solid teak chest of drawers that matched the cupboard and the bed.

"I'm meeting your parents tomorrow," I said.

"You could stay here, if you'd rather," he said glumly. "I could go on my own."

"No," I said, the thought of immediate separation too painful.

And then I cried. Holding back tears so as not to alarm him was irrelevant now. And he comforted me – something he'd been unable to do before. This was a surprise, but it shouldn't have been. He could be kind because I was no longer his responsibility. His freedom had been regained. I was free, too, of course, but I felt as though I was falling in space, that there was no one to hold me, no Catcher in the Rye – or Catcher in the Wry, I might have said in lighter-hearted circumstances – and that there never would be.

Nigel took the next morning off. He and Steven left early to go rock climbing. Rosemary took the morning off, too, and showed me the changes they'd made to the house. The house was an extension of herself, a manifestation of her life with Nigel, and I got immense vicarious pleasure from her pride in it.

The living room and the kitchen on the ground floor were "the hub", as Rosemary put it. The first floor had bedrooms and bathroom; the second, two rooms used as studies; the top floor, an attic with a built-in cupboard.

"You could lock yourself in that cupboard and no one would ever know," I said.

"Why would anyone want to do that?" asked Rosemary.

We went downstairs. Rosemary made breakfast. I looked through the kitchen window at the cottages, some of them hundreds of years old, scattered on the surrounding hills.

"Steven helped us with the deposit on this place, you know," she said, pouring a cup of tea. "We paid it back, of course, but he gave us the money at a time we needed it. We didn't ask him; he offered. He's a good man."

"Yes," I said.

Rosemary leaned forward. I tried to smile, but all I could think of was that I liked her and that I'd probably never see her again. Steven and I would drive to Newcastle in the afternoon. I'd meet his parents and probably never see them again, either.

The rash on my body burned; I thought I could feel it spread. I wanted to put my head on Rosemary's shoulder and tell her I was so distressed I could hardly breathe.

But Rosemary spoke first. "I envy your independence and confidence," she said. "I envy the travel you do and the responsibility you have in your job. Sometimes I think I'm just one of the crowd, that life's passing me by."

I stared at her. "But," I said haltingly, "but everything you . . . what you have . . ."

We heard the front door open, and the heavy tread of boots. A minute later, Nigel and Steven were in the kitchen, smiling like sheepdogs.

"Why can't we just continue as we are?" I asked in the car.

"I wish we could," Steven said. "I've never felt as close to anybody as I've felt to you. But, when I look into the future, I don't see you in it. I wish I did."

I moaned, low, almost a wail, ending in a spasm of sobs. "I'm sorry," I said. "I'm behaving badly."

Steven stared at the road, tears on his face. "No," he said. "You're behaving like a human being."

"I don't know how to fall out of love!"

"Love is only chemicals," he said harshly.

"Do you really believe that?"

"I don't know," he said, less harshly this time.

I thought of all the one-liners I knew about love and pain and the whole damn thing, but humour requires a certain distance, and I couldn't manage it just then. I stared out the window, trying to focus on some point in the future – a future that wouldn't have Steven in it – and conjure an older, wiser

Laurie able to laugh at this younger version falling through space in a car.

I look at that younger Laurie now, all these years later, and I want her back. And I realise, of course, reflecting on what has happened since, that the irony of this story – this spiritual jetlag – is that Peter Pan has turned out to be not Steven but me.

Steven parked in front of a two-storey council house in a 1950s suburb grown comfortable with shrubs and trees. We were late. I donned sunglasses to hide the redness around my eyes.

Steven's mother opened the door. "Hello!" she said, ushering us in. "Laurie, how lovely to meet you."

Steven's father came into the hallway, too. He shook Steven's hand. To me, he smiled and bowed.

The Grotto is a restaurant set into limestone cliffs. From my seat by the window, I watched seagulls swoop around Marsden Rock, lashed by a rough sea.

I couldn't eat. Steven's parents asked me about myself and my work. I tried to be chatty but everything I said merged in my mind with the cries of the gulls. After a while, Steven's parents stopped asking me questions and turned their attention to Steve.

Dessert came, and coffee, then the bill. Steven reached to pick it up but his father wouldn't let him. I looked at the rock one last time.

Framed photographs of Steven hung in the hall, in the sitting room, and on the wall near the stairs. The bowlegged teenager wore soccer shorts. The long-haired graduate clutched an engineering degree. The short-haired graduate held a master's degree in business administration.

I excused myself and went upstairs. The door to what had been Steven's bedroom was open, and I went in. The room was full of squash trophies, soccer pennants, textbooks and posters. I walked to the window, which looked out on the neighbourhood common. What had Steven thought as he'd stood at this window fifteen, twenty years before? Where did he think he'd go? Whom did he think he'd meet?

"Is this where you are, dear!" said Mrs Reid from the doorway. "I've brought you some towels and a nightdress."

"Thank you," I said, taking them and feeling the moist skin of her hands. "Thank you so much."

"Is there anything else you need?"

"No," I said. "You've been very kind." For the second time that day, I had the urge to put my head on the shoulder of a woman I hardly knew.

Steven and his father were walking up the stairs.

In the morning, I woke to find Steven's father in the doorway, holding a cup and saucer. He was dressed in overalls for work.

"What's the point of being a visitor if you don't get tea in bed!" he said.

He put the cup by the bed, smiled, and walked out of the room. I put on the nightdress Mrs Reid had given me and followed Steven's father down the stairs.

"I really enjoyed meeting you," I said awkwardly.

He took my hand and squeezed it. "We hope to see you again soon," he said.

I nodded dumbly.

"Cheerio!" he called before opening the front door.

Steven emerged from the kitchen and shook his hand. I fled upstairs.

After I'd showered, Steven came into the bathroom and said "Hi!" with what I first took to be a valiant attempt at good cheer. But when he got under the shower and started singing a song by Bryan Ferry – another Newcastle boy who had conquered the world – I realised, feeling forlorn, that the high spirits were real.

I dressed, with the sense that I did so in slow motion. When I went to pack, I glanced at Steven's briefcase, which was open on the bed. In one of the pockets was a note in Steven's handwriting, which said:

Thurs 5 July	London – Hong Kong
Fri 6 July	Hong Kong – Sydney
Sat 7 July	Sydney – Auckland
	Week in New Zealand
	Following week in Hong Kong
Sun 22 July	London
Mon & Tues	Scotland, Orion II

He'd underlined Orion II twice, drawn a circle around it, and added a question mark.

What *was* happening with Orion II? Why, given my present sadness, did I even care? But I did. And I caught a glimpse of how Adam and Steven could keep their heads clear for work even when their personal lives were falling apart.

We spent the day in Northumberland, visiting castles whose histories Steven knew in more detail than that provided by tourist pamphlets I bought along the way.

"I used to imagine having grown up in one of these places," he said in the great hall of Bamburgh Castle, where the Celts whose portraits hung high on stone walls could well have been his forebears, with their pale freckled skin and ginger hair.

Steven knew where he came from; his features could be traced. My features could be traced, too, of course, but not in the places I grew up. The features belonged to Jewish villages in Latvia and Lithuania that had been gutted by Cossacks at the end of the nineteenth century. The villages no longer exist. Even if they did, they would be as remote from my experience as castles in Northumberland. The nineteenth and twentieth centuries transplanted so much of the world's population that, for many people, identity is no longer something you're born with but something you have to create.

On the late afternoon flight from Newcastle to London, Steven read through various Orion documents, making comments in the margins. I thought about the sepia-toned photographs my late grandfather had had of family members who had stayed behind in what later became the Soviet Union and who, presumably, had perished during the Second World War.

"A penny for them," Steven said, when trays of tea and biscuits were served.

"I was thinking about the people who came before us," I said, "whose names we don't know but who made us what we are."

Steven glanced at me from beneath lowered eyelids. "I should know better by now than to ask you things like that," he said before busying himself with his tray.

He looked so earnest trying to extricate the biscuits from their plastic wrapping that I smiled.

He smiled, too.

And so, in our room at the Gatwick Hilton, we made love for hours, as though we had a future. I tried to memorise the caress of his fingers in my hair, the pinkness of the skin under his fingernails, and the way his toes curled, as though making a catalogue for a private museum. Which, of course, I was.

In the morning, we had room service coffee and croissants.

At the airport, I waited while Steve checked in at the Cathay Pacific desk for his flight to Hong Kong. Adam was expecting me in the London office at nine.

I walked Steven to the immigration barrier.

"I hate goodbyes," he said.

"Go," I said, kissing him lightly, briefly.

Steven nodded and I watched him walk through.

Adam greeted me at the office with an uncustomary hug. "Well," he said, "you've been to meet the parents. Should I be expecting an announcement?"

"Don't hold your breath."

"Oh," he said.

"So," I said brightly, "I'm here."

"Not for long," said Adam. "You're going to West Berlin. I'll explain on the way to the airport. I'm meeting Frans in Zurich. You're meeting Marthe whatever-her-name-is. My flight leaves an hour before yours."

chapter eleven

At Tegel airport, security guards with guns searched all arriving passengers.

"Is that routine?" I asked Marthe Gerstmann, whose scowl was even deeper than I remembered.

"What?"

"The searches."

"I suppose."

She steered me to the car park, walking so quickly I found it difficult to keep up. She stared at some point in the middle distance, her head pushed forward, the muscles in her neck unnaturally defined.

"I have to tell you about the situation in Düsseldorf," she said, speaking in an almost inaudible monotone.

I closed my eyes in an effort to deflect Marthe's anxiety.

"When I left yesterday afternoon to drive here," she continued, "the tension in the office was cutable like a knife."

I wasn't prepared for this; I hadn't had time to recover from what had happened with Steve. "Can we talk about Düsseldorf later?" I asked.

"Cutable like a knife," Marthe repeated. "Here's my car."

I put my suit-carrier in the back seat, got in the passenger's side, and longed for the quiet, triple-glazed haven of my room at the Hilton. "Did Frans brief you on what we'll be doing here?" I asked, talking slowly in an effort to distance myself from her and focus on business.

"No," she said. "You see, I asked him, and that's the problem."

Clearly, deflection was not going to be possible. "The problem," I said, in a dull echo.

"You can't ask him anything and get a sensible reply, because of the situation in Düsseldorf." She paused and jerked herself forward. "Why won't this car *start*?" She tried the ignition two more times before the engine responded. "All I know is we have an appointment with the research manager of Bartsch Pharmaceuticals."

We had left the airport and were now on the autobahn. Marthe had slowed down at last, perhaps inadvisedly. Cars swished by, hooting to get us out of the way.

"Bartsch bought Orion Constellation two weeks ago," I said. "It's the first sale to a drug company anywhere in the world."

Marthe brightened a little, in spite of herself.

"They've installed it to plan and monitor chemical research, clinical trials – things like that," I said. "There's a huge potential market in the pharmaceutical industry. I did some research on it in Australia."

The pep-talk had started to work on me as well. "Jonathan, no less, has asked for a report. The meeting could be very important – a chance to gain some inside knowledge, to show what you and I can do."

"Do you really think so?" she asked. The car swerved towards the centre of the road.

The Bartsch building was a twelve-storey glass-clad structure not more than 100 metres from the Berlin Wall. The research department had its administrative section on the tenth floor. From the manager's office, you could look out the window clear across East Berlin, at a seemingly unrelieved expanse of grey – streets, apartment blocks, cars, clothes – so different from the gaudiness of the West.

The parallel existence in the one city of two countries, two ideologies, separated by a wall, was bizarre, but was treated with nonchalance by the people in Bartsch, just as now, several years later, German reunification is everyday fact.

I took out my notebook and pen. The manager spoke fluently and well, sometimes in English, sometimes in German which Marthe translated. We made appointments to visit three Bartsch manufacturing plants the following day.

We checked into our hotel and Marthe suggested dinner downstairs. Exhausted, I declined and hoped she would not be too offended.

I had a bath, ordered room service, and watched *Dallas* on TV. The soap opera had been dubbed into German and so my attention was drawn almost exclusively to its visual unfolding. The women – tanned, toned, clothed, coiffed and made-up as Barbie dolls – bared dazzling teeth in expressions that, like those of the men, invariably were hostile. I'd never realised this before: *Dallas* was a place where no one smiled.

I turned off the TV and took a sleeping pill, to turn off me.

In Düsseldorf, after a day at the Bartsch manufacturing plants and a day speaking to clients in Munich and Cologne, I finally accepted Marthe's invitation for dinner. I could not decline for the third night in a row and, in fact, Marthe had been helpful and competent with her translations. Perhaps I had judged her too harshly.

From our table by the window in a restaurant on the Königsalle – an elegant promenade of exclusive boutiques and sumptuous cafes – I watched women with sculpted suits and sculpted hair glide by, as glossy, as polished, as the women in *Dallas*. Did Steven want a woman like that?

"You're not listening," said Marthe.

"Sure I am."

"You're *not*!" And she started to cry.

I stared stupidly at the buttons on Marthe's pale green blouse and felt overcome by fatigue. There simply wasn't any disk space left in my head. When a system approaches overload, it halts.

"You'll have to forgive me," I said. "I'm not concentrating well. Steven and I broke up just before I joined you in Berlin."

"Oh," said Marthe. "I thought you two were virtually married. Why did you break up?"

"He doesn't want me any more," I said, regretting it immediately. I'd made myself vulnerable. Worse than that, I'd allowed the personal to impinge on the professional. Any minute now, Marthe would open the floodgates and pour out what had been preoccupying her for days.

"I don't know what to say," she said.

This statement gave me hope of reprieve. "Tell me what you were trying to tell me before."

Marthe picked up a fork and put it down again. "Frans is having an affair with Frieda."

I looked at her blankly. "Frieda? Who's Frieda?"

"The temporary secretary Frans hired when Christa went on vacation."

I'd never met Christa and I'd not even heard of Frieda. "And?" I asked.

"And he's going to fire Christa so that Frieda can have her job."

"What are you talking about?"

"I just told you!"

"What I mean is, I don't understand the significance of what you're saying."

"He's a liar! A man without scruples!"

"Frans?"

"Of *course* Frans. That's what I'm telling you."

This seemed bewildering to me – extraneous and unnecessarily complicated.

"But you can't just fire someone in Germany," I said. "You've got to prove dishonesty or something, don't you?"

"He'll manage. He doesn't care what he does to get his way."

"Well," I said. "I can see how that strikes you as unfair. But, if things are as you say, there doesn't seem much you can do about it."

"No," said Marthe. "That's why you have to do something about it."

"Me?"

"There's more. Frans also told Frieda that she can have my job in a few months' time."

Marthe's hysteria was washing over me in waves. The only way to counteract it, I thought, was to build up a barrier of some sort, a barricade of reason.

"Does Frieda have your qualifications?" I asked.

"Of course not."

"There you are, then."

"He'll do it!" Marthe said, slumping and crossing her arms. "He'll find a way to do it."

Marthe's panic waves had become tidal. I leaned backwards to try to get out of their way.

"How do you know all this?" I asked.

Marthe uncrossed her arms and leaned across the table. "I heard him tell her," she said.

I felt trapped, on the verge of drowning.

"He always shuts the door to his office when they talk," Marthe continued. "It's the only time he ever shuts his door. Last week, after everyone else had gone home, I listened at the door."

This image was so preposterous, so melodramatic, that I wanted to laugh. But the rabid look in Marthe's eyes made me think better of it. I nodded gravely instead.

"Also," she said, "Frieda goes through the papers on my desk – at night, when there's no one else around."

How much of what Marthe was telling me was true? How much was paranoid delusion?

"How do you know that?" I asked.

"I arrange pencils and paper clips in a particular way. In the morning, they're in different positions."

"Perhaps the cleaning staff move them around," I suggested.

"Cleaning staff come once a week," Marthe replied. She paused. "You don't believe me, do you?"

"I didn't say that."

"You don't know how bad it is," she said, reaching into her handbag. "When Frans has Frieda in there, in the office – sometimes you can't hear any talking at all, they must be kissing or God knows what, it's disgusting, a sixty-year-old married man and a girl like that – everyone else in the office feels uncomfortable. And it's the worst for me because I don't think I will have my job much longer and what will I do then?"

Marthe blew her nose, then wiped her eyes with the back of her hand. "He has all sorts of private meetings with her. She knows everything that's going on in the company – probably things *you* don't even know. The other day, he told her that, if she stuck with him, she wouldn't be sorry, because the company was about to be sold and he'd make a fortune from his shares."

I stared at her and tried to keep my face a mask. *Because the company was about to be sold?* Scenes from the past eighteen months whirred and shuffled in my brain, clicking into a new shape.

Marthe stared back – wildly, madly – and recrossed her arms. "So you're not going to do anything about it," she said.

The waves hit full force now; salt stung my eyes.

"Would you excuse me?" I asked, before fleeing from the table.

In the bathroom, I tried to blot out the image of the waves, rising to the full height of their foam-topped crests before curling over with a terrible beauty and crashing against me.

The implications of the impending sale were overpowering. Right now, though, I had to focus on what to do about Marthe. My first impulse was not to get involved; to finish my contract and get the hell away – from Marthe, from Frans, from Orion, from Steven, from who I'd become.

But to ignore what Marthe had said would be to take the easy way out, to avoid my responsibilities.

This gave me pause. What, exactly, were my responsibilities, and to whom? My brief had been to establish a marketing network for Europe. If something was undermining that network – as Frans's behaviour was or, at least, the way his behaviour was perceived – then it was, indeed, up to me to do something about it.

But what? Confront Frans? Frans and I were barely on speaking terms. Tell Adam? Frans had been Adam's mentor, as Adam had been Steven's, and I'd already seen what could happen when an outsider got wedged in-between.

That led back to the option of doing nothing. But what if "the situation in Düsseldorf", as Marthe kept calling it, got out of hand? What if Adam later discovered that I'd known and had kept it to myself? I would have been negligent – or so it seemed to me. If my loyalties were to the job, and to Adam, I had to tell him.

When I returned to the table, Marthe stood up in a frenzy of seemingly disconnected movements, and I felt a sudden sympathy for her. It was taking all her energy to keep some sort of social and professional persona in place. I could only guess at the deep-seated causes of her distress, but the surface symptoms were evidence enough. "I know how you feel," I said, extending my hand to touch her shoulder.

Marthe jerked her shoulder away. "You don't!" she said. "You're as bad as the men. You don't care what others think. You know what you're doing. No one's threatening you. You're always in control."

"That's not true," I said. "We're all falling apart. Some people just hide it better." I froze at the words, remembering when Steven had said them to me in connection with Susan.

Marthe stared at the carpet as we walked towards the cashier. I handed over my corporate American Express card and was grateful for how long it took the cashier to find the right machine for the card; to get approval from her manager; and to get me to sign. Marthe was silent during this time, and I tried to do some deep breathing exercises without being too obvious.

"We'll talk about this tomorrow, after I've had a look for myself," I said. "I'll help you sort out what's going on, I promise."

Marthe sniffed. "I'll wait and see," she said.

Back at the Rheinstern-Penta Hotel, I stood on the large balcony outside my room and looked at the towers of West German commerce. From the window of the room next door I could hear a loud monologue in Japanese interrupted by brief silences. The man next door appeared to be talking on the phone.

Were things going well for him in Düsseldorf, or badly? Would he return to Tokyo, Osaka or Nagasaki with contracts signed, at terms acceptable to his superiors? What business was he in? Electronics? Textiles? Did he have a family? Did he miss them?

I felt a strong desire to go next door and ask him these things. Instead, I undressed, took off my make-up, and got into bed. In the dark, I listened to the one-sided conversation on the other side of the wall. The voice of a faceless Japanese businessman would be one of the key elements in my memory of this night yet I'd never know his name.

The next morning I made lists and organised notes, this time from the interviews in Berlin, Munich and Cologne. Marthe did the same, until we heard Frans greet Frieda at reception. He came in, said a formal hello to me, then returned to the reception area and ushered Frieda into his office, closing the door.

"*See?*" said Marthe. She got up and, in the spirit of a four-year-old, threw the Bartsch annual report on the floor. "I'm not going to give Frieda any more letters to type or . . . or . . . *anything*," she said. "I'm *not*. I'm going to completely ignore her."

Marthe sat down. I picked up the report and put it back on the desk. "Ignoring her will simply make you upset," I said. "Why give her that power? She doesn't have your qualifications. She doesn't have your ability. She won't get your job."

"What's to stop her?" Marthe demanded. "Frans already gave her Christa's job."

I looked up. Frieda was at the door, watching us slyly, through half-closed eyes and a haze of cigarette smoke. From *Dallas* to art films, I thought.

"Frans said you should tell me about the marketing plans so that I can help," she said.

Marthe glared at me.

I looked at Frieda as coolly as Frieda was looking at me. "So you're interested in marketing?"

"Yes," she said. "Frans says we should all try to improve ourselves."

"Why don't you fetch another chair?" I said slowly, planning what to say. "Marthe and I will explain. Marthe, of course, will be doing all the work herself, but it would be good for you to have a general understanding when you're typing her reports."

Frieda was annoyed. She tottered out of the room on spiky heels, returning with a chair.

"I wonder if you'd mind extinguishing your cigarette?" I asked.

"A lot of people smoke in this office," Frieda said. "Frans smokes."

"I know that. But Marthe and I don't. I wonder if you'd mind putting it out?"

Frieda stared at me defiantly. I stared back. Finally, she took one last drag and stubbed out the cigarette on a piece of paper which she put in the bin. She sat down.

I'd won round one. In round two, I outlined our strategy for Germany using rather more marketing jargon than necessary. Panic crept into Frieda's hostile stare, but Marthe did not seem to comprehend what I was trying to do. She sat with her shoulders hunched and would not stir.

Afterwards, Frieda went back to reception and Marthe and

I went out for lunch, but not before Marthe had arranged the objects on her desk.

Lunch was a high-strung affair, Marthe saying little; which I found preferable to being buffeted by waves of despair. When we got back, I could see that the objects on Marthe's desk were, indeed, in different positions.

"Laurie?" Frans called from the door. "Would you come into my office?"

I got up. Marthe busied herself with a pencil sharpener.

Frans closed the door of his office after I'd entered and, without looking at me, invited me to sit down. He picked up an Orion paperweight and dispensed with preliminaries. "I had to fire Christa because she was unstable," he said. "Frieda is a better secretary."

"What has this got to do with me?" I asked.

"I'm telling you this because Marthe seems to have taken a dislike to Frieda." Frans put down the paperweight. "She was quite friendly, on the other hand, with Christa. As I said, Christa was not very stable. I don't think Marthe is so stable herself."

Only then did he look at me, with an expression that was almost a challenge. A challenge to do or say what?

"We'll have reports on our visits in Munich and Cologne ready tomorrow," I said. "The report on Bartsch will take a few days longer. Marthe is doing some translation for me. Her translation skills are good."

"Yes, yes," Frans said. He picked up the paperweight and waved it at me, which I took as a cue I could go.

Marthe lived in a stylish, ordered, sparsely furnished apartment where the bedroom was partitioned from the living room by black metal bookshelves.

"I've got a quiche," she said. "It won't take long to warm up. Make yourself comfortable."

I sat down on a peach-coloured couch, not being comfortable at all. I would rather have been at the Rheinstern-Penta watching *Dallas* in German or listening to my neighbour talk in Japanese on the phone. Here I was instead, in a Düsseldorf suburb, trying to be a good manager.

I got up and crossed the room to inspect the shelves. The books were filed alphabetically, German and English together. I scanned the names – Erikson, Freud, Fromm, Horney, Jung, Klein, Kohut, Maslow, Miller, Reik.

Marthe emerged from the kitchen with the quiche. "Where did you study psychology?" I asked.

She put down the quiche. "I didn't. My degree was in marketing. Did you study psychology?"

"No," I said, and laughed nervously. I'd read many of the books on Marthe's shelves, too. People widely read in psychoanalytic thought are not so by accident. There were places in Marthe that I didn't have the strength to visit. There were enough places with which to contend of my own. I hoped we'd be able to get through the evening on as friendly but superficial a place as possible.

We sat down at a peach-coloured table and Marthe cut the quiche. We ate a slice each in silence.

"Your quiche is excellent," I said. "May I have another piece?"

"I'll give you the recipe," she said and, instead of cutting me another slice, got up and went to the kitchen, where she consulted a neat file of index cards. She extricated the one with the recipe and also an unmarked card.

Returning to the table with the cards and a pen, she sat down and wrote out the recipe for me, translating it into English as she went.

"Thanks," I said, when she'd finished and handed the English version to me. "Thanks," I said again, when she handed me another slice of quiche. I surreptitiously looked at my watch and wondered when I'd be able to leave without appearing rude.

But then she started to cry. "I want a career where I'm getting somewhere!" she said. "I want a long-term job where I can do some good things! How can I feel secure with Frieda around? How can I achieve anything in a situation like that? How can I amount to anything in a situation like that?"

The black metal bookshelves closed in on me — a giant, menacing, hi-tech geometric web. I wasn't going to be able to escape, after all. And so I listened for hours, to an increasingly incoherent tale about two fathers and three boyfriends; a breakdown at university and a year repeated; a first job with a market research company and then the job with Orion and the problem with Frans. All I could do was nod and wait for a suitable juncture to leave.

By midnight, I was finally on my own, back at the hotel, feeling wrung-out and numb. Images of Marthe mixed with images of Susan and — something which startled me — with images of my mother, whose alternating distance and rage I'd had to accommodate in my life but had never really questioned. I started to feel frightened, as though these images were going to engulf me. Slowly, methodically, I hung up my clothes, brushed my teeth, took off my make-up, then dialled 852 for Hong Kong.

"I'm sorry to wake you," I said.

"What time is it? Seven o'clock. The alarm's about to go off any minute anyway. How are you?"

Now that we were no longer together, Steven was more polite than he'd ever been. "Fine," I said, "and you?"

"Fighting fit."

"I'm sorry to disturb you – "

"Stop apologising. You can ring any time you want."

"I need to talk to somebody. There's something weird going on here and I don't know how to handle it. You're the only person I can discuss it with."

"Shoot."

I told him about Frans and Frieda, but something made me hold back on what Frans had said about Orion's looming sale.

"Are you sure Marthe is telling the truth?" Steve asked.

"I was dubious at first, too. But she probably is."

"You have to tell Adam."

"That's what I thought. But you know as well as I do what sort of relationship Adam has with Frans. Where will that leave me? It will be Lucy all over again."

"It will not. It's entirely different. It's not a case of poaching staff. It's a question of withholding information."

"That was my conclusion, too."

"You have to tell him."

"Yes."

"Let me know how it pans out."

"I will."

"I'd better get up. What's the weather like over there?"

"Gorgeous," I said. To be honest, I'd hardly noticed.

"You don't realise how lucky you are to be out of Hong Kong. This July has been even worse than last year. The air outside is like soup. That's how you used to describe it, isn't it? Hundred-degree soup."

"Double, double toil and trouble," I said.

"What?"

"The witches in *Macbeth*."

"*What?*"

"The cauldron. Hundred-degree soup."

Steven was silent. "I miss you sometimes," he said.

"Sometimes."

"Laurie – "

"You'd better get up," I said, replacing the mouthpiece in its cradle and, with it, the sad images of Marthe, Susan, my mother and another woman, whom I dimly recognised as myself.

Adam telephoned me next morning before I'd had a chance to think about what I should tell him or when.

"I'd like you back here tomorrow morning," he said. "Jonathan wants a progress report on marketing staff and I need to talk to you about it. Could you get here by eleven o'clock?"

"Sure," I said. "There are a couple of things I need to talk to you about, too."

Ellen's scowl as she bent over her typewriter was similar to Marthe's when I'd told her I was returning to Gouda. "You're not going to do anything about the situation at all!" she'd said. I'd told her I'd talk to Adam, but the response had been bunched eyebrows and lowered lids.

"Hi," I said to Ellen. "I have a meeting with Adam at eleven."

"I don't know anything about that," Ellen said. "In any case, he has people with him."

"He set a time for eleven. Will you buzz me?"

At midday, I returned to Ellen's desk.

"He's still in the meeting," she said.

"When will he be free?"

"When he's finished."

"When will he be finished?"

"When he's free."

Was this a parody of *Catch-22* or did she genuinely think like this? Why did Adam put up with her? I knew the answer to that, of course: because Frans had brought her with him.

I went back to my desk. Brian Sedgwick was hanging up his jacket. "Do I know you?" he asked.

"You can talk!"

"At least you've been somewhere reasonable," he said. "I've just spent the week in Riyadh because the support person who was meant to be handling a problem there got thrown in jail. Home brewing."

"Not another one!"

"So he'll have to leave Saudi when they release him, and I'll have to go through all that procedure of installing a replacement." Brian looked at his watch. "Adam said twelve o'clock."

"He's in a meeting. I had an appointment with him at eleven."

Brian went to talk to Ellen. When he came back, he said: "What *is* it, with that woman?"

"I think she sees us as the enemy."

"Why?"

I shrugged. "Her loyalty is to Frans. She thinks our loyalty is to Adam."

"It is."

"QED."

Brian sat down and started tapping his foot. "I've got enough problems without having to put up with – "

"I know. I'll make some tea."

"Thanks," he said. "I didn't mean to take it out on you."

At one o'clock, Brian asked Ellen if Adam was free yet. At two o'clock, I asked her. At two thirty, Brian said: "I'm supposed to be in Eindhoven by half past three. Will you tell Adam I waited?"

"Of course."

At three o'clock, Adam was still busy.

At four thirty, Ellen said: "He left half an hour ago to get the plane to Paris."

"But he called me *back* here!" I said.

"*I* don't know anything about that," she said.

"I got your message when I arrived at the hotel," Adam said on the phone.

I was sitting in my room at the Schiphol Hilton. "You arranged a meeting for eleven o'clock."

"Oh hell. Sorry. I didn't write it down."

"You had a meeting with Brian, too."

"Is he back from Saudi?"

"He waited until half past two."

"I must write things down. Can you handle that staffing report for Jonathan on your own?"

"It's done," I said. "I'll fax it to you tomorrow."

"Can you ring me before you do? I'd rather Jean-Claude didn't see it."

"Sure."

"Well that's fine, then."

"Yes."

"Good."

"Adam, there's something I feel I ought to tell you. I wanted to tell you in person, but – "

"What?"

"It's sort of delicate. I would prefer if you kept it in confidence – that is, if you would not directly confront the party concerned, but just be aware of what's happening."

"Of course."

I told him about Frans and Frieda but omitted, once again – some survival instinct told me to – what Frans had said about the proposed sale.

"Thank you for telling me," Adam said, in a flat, uninflected voice.

"It's Adam," said Annelies.

I picked up the phone.

"I can't speak long," he said. "I have to leave to catch a flight to London. But I talked to Frans."

I shut my eyes and clutched at the edge of the desk. Adam had ignored my request and I could see what lay ahead. Massive waves crashed in my head and the beginnings of a rash appeared on my arms. But I was not surprised, and that made me even more angry – at Adam, for his predictable behaviour; at myself, for trying to do the right thing by Adam yet knowing what would happen; and at Steven, for falsely allaying my fears.

"Frans called Marthe into the office," he continued, "and we cleared up the whole misunderstanding."

I sat there, numb and drenched in sweat. When Adam had finished, I put down the phone and waited for Marthe to call.

"Things are worse now!" she wailed. "Frans hauled me into his office in front of Adam and demanded to know if I thought he was having an affair with Frieda. He said you said he was. He said the whole idea was ridiculous because she's twenty-eight and he's sixty. He's a liar. He's – "

"What did *you* say?"

"What *could* I say? I said I didn't know if he was having an affair with Frieda or not, and that it was none of my business. But now everyone's suspicious of me! It's unbearable."

"You'll have to pull yourself together," I said. "I did what you asked, and now you've put me in a very difficult position."

"Frieda's going to get my job, not yours!"

"Did you mention your fears about this?"

"Of course I didn't."

"Or what Frans told Frieda about the sale?"

"Why would I do that?"

The waves were everywhere now. Months of rage broke free.

"It's the worst possible outcome," I said. "Why can't Adam learn to keep his mouth shut?"

"I thought Adam would be harder on Frans than that," Steven said. "Frans is behaving like an idiot. I don't know why this surprises me. He *is* an idiot."

"Frans doesn't know when to keep his mouth shut, either," I said. "Are you aware that he's going around telling people in the Düsseldorf office that the company's about to be sold?"

"Are you sure?" Steven's voice was very deep.

"Of course I'm sure."

"Now that *is* silly. *Very* silly. Very, *very* silly." Steven sounded almost gleeful. "Where's Adam right now?"

"In the air. Düsseldorf–London."

"I'll be in London in a few days' time."

"Again?"

"Jonathan has called another meeting."

"Then talk of a sale must be true."

Steven was silent.

"You owe me an answer!"

"Yes it is. But I'm asking you as a personal favour to keep it quiet. We can't afford to have widespread panic."

"Who's the buyer?"

Steven hesitated.

"*Who's the buyer?*"

"An American aerospace company."

"That gives me a shortlist at least," I said sarcastically.

"I can't bring myself to tell you any more than that. I've told you more than I should have already."

"How long have you known this?"

"Not that long, really."

"*How long have you known this?*"

"Officially, since Christmas. But I had my suspicions before."

"Why didn't you tell me?"

"It wasn't possible."

This made me feel so agitated that my arms and legs began to make small, quick movements outside my control, and my head felt as though it were expanding. "But how do you think I *feel?*" I said. "Everything I've done for the company has been totally meaningless."

"Not true," Steven said. "As a matter of fact, some of it was pretty damn useful."

"But for reasons I wasn't told about!" I thought back on the client surveys I'd done in Asia, the market research I'd done in Australia, and the creation of a marketing network in Europe. All these things had been done not to build up Orion but to pretty it for sale.

I remembered Steven's response to my question in that hateful room at the Marriott. "What is there in Scotland that everyone's trying to hide?" I'd asked. "Nothing," he'd replied.

Things were falling into place. What did Orion have to sell? An existing product, a customer base, a network of staff. That was half of it. The other half was the potential to remain the leader in its field, which meant research and development. Research and development, in Orion, meant Orion Constellation II. And Orion Constellation II meant the castle in Scotland, which no one was allowed to go near.

"I've been manipulated," I said.

"Yes," said Steven. "You've been manipulated by Marthe."

"That's not what I meant, and you know it," I said. "But, talking of that, *you* told me to tell Adam."

"I didn't know Adam would handle it so badly." Steven paused. "I'm partly responsible for what's happened. Laurie, I'm really sorry." He paused again. "After the meeting with Jonathan in London, I think I'll go to the Lake District for a few days. I need to get away. You do, too. Will you come?"

"You can't be serious."

"Oh, Laurie, I know. But I am. I'd like you to come. We could go walking a lot and just be good to each other."

"You really can't be serious."

"We can take it as it comes. I could drive to Manchester from London and meet you at the airport on Wednesday afternoon. You could be back in Holland on Monday. That means you'd lose less than three days' work. You work that in overtime every couple of weeks anyway. Adam will agree. I'll make sure he agrees."

"Will your house be available?"

"No. It's booked until October. We can stay with Nigel and Rosemary."

"That will surprise them."

"Nothing surprises them about me any more."

"Steven – "

"Where will you be next week?"

"Oslo."

"Shouldn't be too difficult to get to Manchester from there. Will you come?"

I should have said no. "Yes," I said.

chapter twelve

When I walked through the arrival doors at Manchester airport, Steven wasn't there. I laughed. "I *meant* to be on time," he'd say. "I *meant* to, honest, but Adam was in the office – " And I would smile.

At one of the small formica-topped tables in the hall, I unfurled a copy of *The Guardian* I'd bought at Fornebu airport while waiting for the plane. It was several days old so I skipped the news and turned to the feature pages.

"Misfit in a world of freaks" was the headline below a photograph of Diane Arbus, the photographer who chronicled the lives of American outcasts and who committed suicide, an outcast herself. "A photograph is a secret about a secret," she once said. "The more it tells you the less you know."

I stared at the photograph of Arbus, in Central Park, April 1967, four years before her death. Her camera was slung around her neck – her window and her noose.

My typewriter was in my briefcase.

What if a photograph was taken of me at this moment – what would it show? A young woman in a business suit reading a newspaper in an airport cafeteria. I scrutinised this imaginary photograph in my mind. The more I examined it, the less I knew.

More than an hour had passed. Where *was* he? I rang Nigel and Rosemary to see if Steven had left a message there. "No," said Rosemary, "but you know Steve!"

Half an hour after that, I asked the woman at the Avis

counter to enquire if an accident had been reported. She telephoned the Avis emergency number. "No," she said, after putting down the phone. "No report."

Now I was angry. Would Steven ever allow himself to be late to meet the flight of a colleague or a client?

I called Rosemary again. "If Steven calls," I said, "or when he arrives, tell him I've gone home, to Amsterdam."

"You can't just get on a plane like it's a bus!" Rosemary said and handed me over to Nigel.

"He's just a little late," Nigel said. "I don't understand why you're so upset."

How could I explain that Steven's failure to be there when he'd said he would was symbolic of just about everything?

There was, indeed, a flight to Amsterdam, but I didn't book a seat. I paced around the small arrival area – sometimes listless, sometimes agitated, waiting, *waiting*.

By four o'clock, my anger had reverted to concern. I asked the Avis woman to enquire again. She was on the phone when Steven walked through the doors from the car park.

The woman put down the receiver.

Steven tried to smile. He tentatively held out his arms.

"You're more than two hours late," I said.

"I *meant* to be on time," he said. "I *meant* to, honest, but Adam was in the office . . . Why are you staring?"

"I'm relieved you weren't in an accident. Now I'm flying back to Amsterdam."

"But you're *here*."

"*You* should have been, too."

"I *am* here now. Please stay."

I'd never been able to say no to Steven. I loved him too much, or couldn't bear the thought of separation. It's not the same thing – I know that now – but it has always felt so to me.

And so we made our way to the Lake District in another hired Mercedes, and I despaired that the only means I seemed to have of reaching Steven was to make threats I never carried through.

"I think you should speak to Adam," Steven said. "He's a bit put out. Something about a meeting in Paris you arranged without his consent, and something else about Düsseldorf."

"Bloody *Adam*!" I said. "I've been leaving messages for Adam all over the place for *days*. In the end, I made a decision without him. I have to get the European and Scandinavian marketing staff together in one place for a meeting, and Paris has the best flight connections. As for Düsseldorf, that has taken on a nightmare life of its own – very largely, if I may say so, because of how ineptly Adam handled it."

"A few things need to be cleared up," Steven said. "I do feel partly responsible. I've said that before."

We drove the rest of the way in silence.

"No seats to Amsterdam available, then?" Nigel asked, taking my bags.

Steven laughed, his smooth-things-over laugh. "I've been meaning to talk to you about Amsterdam, lad. We should arrange a climbing expedition in the Dutch mountains."

"The Dutch mountains?" asked Nigel. "Oh, the Dutch *mountains*. Yes, even Rosemary and Laurie would probably be able to manage climbing in the Dutch mountains."

"My particular specialty," I said, trying to follow Steve's lead in mitigating the embarrassment I'd caused, "is making mountains out of molehills."

Rosemary laughed. "We thought for a moment you *meant* it," she said.

"I did."

Steven's shoulders slumped. Rosemary slapped me on the arm. "You *Australians!*" she said, and we all went inside.

"It's for you, lad," Nigel said after dinner, holding out the phone. Steven walked across the kitchen with apple cake and a cup of tea.

Rosemary was talking about the flowers they'd planted that spring. I nodded politely, trying to keep an ear on Steven's conversation. It sounded routine – budgets and targets – until a long silence, after which Steven said: "I don't think that's quite right, Adam. Laurie told me she tried to contact you for days about that meeting, and that you didn't return her calls. What you said about Frans doesn't sound quite right, either. If Laurie says something is the case, then that's the case. She's got no reason for a vendetta against Frans."

"Excuse me," I said, getting up from the table, with a rising sense of anger and desperation.

Steven passed me the phone.

"Adam," I said, "I must have rung you fifteen times about the Paris meeting. I'll talk about that in a minute. About Frans, I certainly didn't expect you to confront him and tell him *I* had made the allegations about Frieda. I simply told you what had happened so that you would know. Steve said it would be wrong not to tell you."

"I didn't appreciate the fact that you talked to Steven about it."

"You can't expect me not to talk to Steven, for heaven's sake."

Steven took the phone again and started chewing the nails of his left hand – something I hadn't seen him do since Singapore. Rosemary and Nigel had their heads down. They cut their slices of cake into smaller and smaller pieces.

"Now you shut up for a change and *listen*," Steven said to Adam, his voice as low as I'd ever heard it. "I made Laurie tell you about Frans. I take responsibility for it and I would make the same decision again. So you should put some of the blame on me. And you should put some of the blame on yourself, too, for handling everything so bloody badly."

Steven bit his nails as he listened to Adam's reply. "Here," he said, handing me the phone.

"Let's speak on Tuesday, back in the office," Adam said, his voice quieter now.

"What about the meeting in Paris?" I asked, my voice quieter now, too.

"Of course you should have the meeting, but could you have it in Gouda? I'd like to be there."

"I'll change the arrangements."

"Goodbye, then," Adam said, his voice tight.

"Goodbye."

I put down the phone. Steven and I stood facing each other. Rosemary and Nigel scrupulously sipped tea.

"Frans is a bastard through and through," Steven said, not looking at me. "He walks into the company from outside, gets all those shares for having done absolutely bugger all, then makes his own rules about how to behave. I don't know who the hell he thinks he is."

I stared at him. "Is *that* why – " I said. I wanted to hit him, to scream, cry or run out of the room. Instead, I stood there angry to the point of paralysis.

"Your tea's getting cold," Rosemary said.

"This is Gunner's How," Steven said, as I scrambled to keep up with his ascent of it. All the hills in the Lake District seemed to have impenetrable names like this. I had stopped asking why.

When Steven reached the peak, he stood with his hands in the pockets of his jacket and looked out over Lake Windermere. He stood there so totally and happily on his own that I held back, not wanting to intrude.

I looked down, at what was probably one of the most beautiful views in the world. But all I could think about was Frans, Frieda and Marthe; about the ethical implications of the proposed Orion sale; and about this silent man with wind in his eyes.

Steven sat at the kitchen table with the usual batch of memos, the morning sun bleaching his face. I retreated to Nigel's study with notes on Bartsch Pharmaceuticals I'd been carrying around for almost two weeks. But Steven came upstairs, and we went walking.

I tried to write the report the following morning, and the one after that, but I couldn't come up with a first sentence. Patently, this was ridiculous.

But Steven had been more considerate, more polite, than I would have thought possible. He'd even made love politely, as though nothing was at stake. We were due to leave next day for Manchester, where I'd fly to Amsterdam and Steven would take the shuttle to Heathrow for a flight to Hong Kong. Our relationship would end, finally, with nothing having been said to mark its passing.

"Hi!" said Steve in the doorway. "Ready for a walk?"

"I really have to finish this report."

"Seems to be taking rather a long time. Sure you won't come?"

I nodded.

"Never mind. I'll pick you up at six. The estate agent said we can have access to my house between six thirty and seven thirty, after the old tenants leave, before the new ones arrive."

"Fine."

"See you then!"

He bounded down the stairs. I stared at my notes. I'd been looking forward to seeing this house for months. It had become almost mythical – a place to be with Steven where Steven felt most himself. But what was the point of seeing the house now?

I heard Steven collect his walking boots from our bedroom. A minute or so later, I heard the front door swing shut.

Nigel and Rosemary were at work. I stared again at my notes. The report should have taken no more than two or three hours to write. But what was it *for*? One more document to back up Orion's "potential". One more document to make Jonathan, Ted, Adam, Steven, Frans and a few others rich. I'd been kidding myself about my role in Orion. I'd been kidding myself about Steven, too.

A cloud of self-loathing and disgust lowered itself over my head, spreading like the rash I still had to smooth make-up on every morning to conceal. This was it, then – the thing I had refused to confront.

I tidied up my notes with a sudden sense of clarity and calm, and walked lightly up the stairs. The attic was as bare as I remembered. I opened the cupboard, got in, and closed the door behind me. The door fitted snugly.

I closed my eyes. I was in a cupboard in an attic in a large and solidly built empty house on a large block of land at the end of an English village.

The realisation that I could suffocate in here made me shake my head self-mockingly. That wasn't what I had intended. What, then? Well, I could scream. I could scream, let everything out, then go downstairs and start to put my life into some sort of order.

But when I tried to scream, nothing came out. I tried again. All that emerged was a half-strangled cry that sounded like a distant bird. And I remembered something Susan had said: "You know what the worst thing is? When you want to scream and you can't."

"I care about you," I'd said.

"Why?"

"Because you're my friend."

"But I'm not the same person any more."

"You will be."

Susan had turned her face, a stranger's face. "How?" she'd asked.

It was getting hot, here in the cupboard, and difficult to breathe. I flung the door open and ran out of the attic, down the stairs to the study, down the stairs to the bedrooms below, down the stairs to the living room, all the way to the front door where, puffing with exertion, I opened the door and stared at the sun.

Steven's house was in one of the newer subdivisions of Ambleside. It did not have the charm of the older houses in the village, of course, but it was comfortable and, from the back, overlooked some hills.

"Isn't it terrific?" he asked from the back porch. "Isn't it a great place to be?"

In the car – on this, our last night in the Lake District – Steven said: "I'm really glad you saw the house."

"Why?"

"Because I wanted you to see it."

I looked out the window at a marina with billboards saying

Boats For Hire. He was glad I'd seen the house because he'd wanted me to see it. What sort of answer was that?

"You belong in politics," I said. It was a throwaway line but he took it seriously.

"No," he said. "Not enough control."

"Control?"

"Politicians are at the mercy of too many unpredictable external factors. There are external factors in business, too, but you usually have a pretty good idea of what they are."

"You have to control everything!" I said.

Steven stopped by the side of the road and looked at me. I was as shaken at my outburst as he was. "The problem with our relationship," I said, "is that you feel you can't control me." (This wasn't what I really meant. What I meant was that I couldn't control me.)

"What brought this on?"

"It is, isn't it?" I demanded stubbornly.

"I've never said that."

"No, and that's another part of the problem," I said, feeling a rhythm build. "You avoid saying anything until you absolutely have to. You avoid everything. You stay in control. We've been so polite to each other these past few days, we haven't even acknowledged what has happened."

I covered my eyes in embarrassment and remorse.

"If I felt I loved you as much as it's possible to love someone," he said, "I wouldn't think twice. But I just don't. I wish I did."

There was no way to counter this. There was nothing I could do or say that would change this – ever. "You're right to be honest," I said. "I'm behaving badly."

"You're behaving like a human being."

The sobs came, inevitably, and I could not contain them. "I had a future in mind," I said. "It's hard to let go. I hate how I'm behaving. I hate being the hurt, helpless female. It's demeaning. It's out of control."

"That word again," Steven said. "But why do you want to change? You have feelings. You let yourself have feelings. You don't try to pretend you don't have any, like I do."

"What's the point of having feelings if it means you can't function properly? I don't know if I can hold together."

Steven touched my arm. "Everyone has periods when they feel like that," he said. "I felt like that in Singapore. A new job. Not knowing where I was with it. Not being able to spend enough time with the staff. Not being able to spend enough time with you. Not being able to decide yes, no, sorry, maybe."

This made me feel more ashamed than ever. I'd been so wrapped up in my own needs during our time in Singapore, I'd never really tried to look at things through Steve's eyes.

"I hope – " I said quietly. "I hope, on balance, that I was more of a help than a hindrance."

"Yes," said Steven, but not without hesitating.

He started the car again and left the main road for a complicated detour to reach a shop he knew which sold ice-cream. When we arrived, he stopped and got out of the car.

He returned with two cones of ice-cream – one chocolate, one strawberry – and held them out to me. "Choose, beautiful," he said.

The alarm clock rang at 6 a.m. Neither of us had slept much. I had spent most of the night in tears, alternately allowing Steven to hold me then pushing him away. But when the alarm went off, I hugged him tightly, for what really would be, now, the last time.

We got out of bed sluggishly, to shower, dress and pack. I

watched Steven smooth out a pair of trousers on a flat plastic hanger and clip the hanger into its special place in the suit-carrier.

"I'm sick of all this packing," he said. "I'd like to stay in one place for a while."

"So would I," I said in a strangled voice. I would like to have stayed in one place for a while with Steve.

We left a note for Rosemary and Nigel, who were still asleep, and drove to Manchester airport in silence. Steve returned the keys to the Avis desk. The woman remembered us and could not hide her curiosity. I tried to stand outside myself, to take an imaginary photograph.

I checked in at the KLM desk. Steven got a ticket for the British Airways super shuttle to Heathrow.

A woman's voice came through on the loudspeaker. "Will passengers on flight KL154 to Amsterdam please proceed to gate number four."

This was unfair. My heart was breaking and now I was going to play out a scene everyone has seen too many times in too many films.

We walked to the departure gates together, arms around each other, briefcases in our spare hands. At the sign indicating international departures to the right, UK flights to the left, we hugged, wordlessly, before going our separate ways.

Everything that happened after that was postscript.

In the showdown with Frans and Adam in Gouda, Frans at first refused to let me talk. Adam punched the table and said: "Now, shut up for a change and *listen*."

Frans finally listened.

"I tried to do the right thing," I said. "It wasn't a personal vendetta."

"We all behaved badly, I suppose," Frans said, after a while.

"Yes, we did," Adam said.

The reports were written, the sales brochures prepared, and a shortlist of candidates drawn up for my job (which went, in the end, after all the forays outside the company, to Jean-Claude Mabire).

Marthe was fired. Frieda was promoted to take her place and was fired six months later. She demanded a large severance payment for wrongful dismissal, which Adam agreed to after Frans admitted that everything Marthe – and I – had said was true.

While I was at Columbia University, Orion Management Systems was sold to Wheeldon Baxter International for one hundred and twenty million pounds. I read the news in *The Wall Street Journal* and rang Graham Danvers in Singapore. He told me that the figure had been arrived at as being sixty million pounds for the company at the time of sale and sixty million pounds for the potential of Orion Constellation II.

Much of the money went to Jonathan Grosvenor and Ted Jennings, but Frans Timmerman, Adam Sarris and Steven Reid came out multi-millionaires as well. All were required by the sale agreement to remain with the company for three years, as were the second tier of management, all of whom had made modest fortunes from their own Orion shares.

Sales plateaued.

"It wasn't the same," Graham said. "Working for Orion became just another job."

I graduated from Columbia with respectable honours and joined the staff of a Manhattan-based business magazine.

Orion Constellation II was officially scrapped eighteen months after the sale. Graham rang to tell me. "There never *was* an Orion Constellation II – not seriously," he said.

Three years after the sale, Jonathan bought a farm in Sussex and became a recluse. Ted Jennings became a Born Again Christian and set up a non-profit charity foundation. Frans, Adam and Steven left as soon as their contractual obligations had been discharged, to start a company offering management and software application advice to large corporations. They took Max James, Lucy and Ian Phillips with them.

Graham joined a Singapore-based computer applications firm. Roger Benham, Dick Staunton, Christopher Kendall and all the other people I had worked with along the way found senior jobs in companies involved with computers or went out on their own as consultants.

Orion Constellation lost its position as market leader. Wheeldon Baxter International sold off its Orion division less than a year after Frans, Adam and Steven had left, for forty-two million pounds less than they'd paid.

I returned to Melbourne after seeing a series of Qantas ads that made me homesick for Australia. But I realised, almost as soon as I'd collected my bags at Tullamarine airport, that I'd made a mistake. There was no one there connected to me in any meaningful way other than Susan, and Susan had become a passive, *absent* person who stared at nothing in particular. When I visited her – she was living with her parents – she did not know who I was.

I came back here, to Amsterdam, wondering how many more times in my life I'd have to go somewhere else.

My apartment, on the third floor of an eighteenth-century house, overlooks a canal where ducks splash and swans glide gracefully past houseboats. I work as a freelance writer for various British and American business magazines. I like Amsterdam, and the small circle of friends I've made, but life seems less compelling somehow. Perhaps it's simply a function of growing older; I don't know.

I still wonder, sometimes, how the people in Orion got away with selling a company on the basis of a non-existent second version of its product.

Graham turned up in Amsterdam not long ago, to take part in a computer show, and I asked him.

"It was a very convincing play," he said. "Good script, good direction, some good performances from leading actors, good sets, good props. All it needed was an audience – which Wheeldon Baxter provided."

"And a few minor characters like me."

Graham laughed. "It's not whether you win or lose," he said, "but where you lay the blame."

I laughed, too – finally, after all these years – and decided to let him have the last word.

Founded in 1986, Serpent's Tail publishes the innovative and the challenging.

If you would like to receive a catalogue of our current publications please write to:

FREEPOST
Serpent's Tail
4 Blackstock Mews
LONDON N4 2BR

(No stamp necessary if your letter is posted in the United Kingdom.)